Felonious Felines

Other Five Star Titles
by Ed Gorman:

Night Kills

FELONIOUS FELINES

Edited by Carol and Ed Gorman

Five Star
Unity, Maine

Five Star First Edition Mystery Series.
Published in 2000 in conjunction with Tekno Books & Ed Gorman.

Cover design by Carol Pringle.

Set in 11 pt. Plantin by Rick Gundberg.

Printed in the United States on permanent paper.

Library of Congress Cataloging-in-Publication Data

Felonious felines / edited by Carol and Ed Gorman.
    p.   cm. — (Five Star first edition mystery series)
   ISBN 0-7862-2689-7 (hc : alk. paper)
   1. Cats — Fiction. 2. Detective and mystery stories, American.
I. Gorman, Carol. II. Gorman, Edward. III. Series.
PS648.C38 F45 2000
  813′.087208362952—dc21   00-034754

Table of Contents

Introduction

Ed Gorman

As I've noted before, mystery writers loved to be photographed with their cats. Raymond Chandler, Erle Stanley Gardner, even tough-guy Mickey Spillane . . . all have an affinity for the sweet-natured, intelligent, always obedient, and generally swell-to-the-highest-power creatures who run our daily lives.

So it's only right that we dedicate an entire collection to them in all their splendor . . . and mysterious ways. For if there's one thing cats are . . . it's mysterious. Ask the ancient Egyptians who idolized them as gods. Ask the folks of Salem, Mass. who saw them as soldiers in Satan's army. Or ask anybody who has ever crossed a street so as to avoid a black cat.

Now you and I know better than all this nonsense. We know there's nothing mysterious at all about cats. They like to eat, sleep, yawn, run up and down stairs, and groom themselves. And that's about all they like to do, when you come right down to it. Because they're special beings and they know it. They leave the tricks and the showing-off to dogs. All they want is a house where they're in total command . . . and then they'll leave us humans pretty much alone.

Carol and I hope you like this book. We had a great time reading stories for it. And we took the best of them and put them between these covers.

So, here's to happy reading.

I hope you'll excuse me. I haven't fed our cats in nearly an hour and they're starting to pick up those little .45s we got them for Christmas . . .

—Ed Gorman

Dr. Couch Saves a Cat

Nancy Pickard

"It may seem terrible," the old veterinarian admitted to his granddaughter, "that I was so worried about a cat when there was a person who had just passed on. But it was an awfully nice cat, and the human being wasn't much to brag about, I'm sorry to say."

"Tell me about the cat, Grandpa."

"A child after my own heart."

The old man smiled at the ten-year-old whose hair was the same shade of shiny walnut that his had been seventy years ago and who was a stringbean, as he had been in his youth, and who also had inherited his unusual shade of light brown eyes. Her name was Frances—which she hated, except for the fact that she was named after him—and so she went by Frankie. His name was Franklin Couch. Everybody except the child—even his own daughters, sometimes—called him Dr. Frank. He was a formal sort of man with most people, a trait he deeply regretted when he gauged the emotional distance between him and his daughters. With animals and small children, however, he was magic. Butterflies landed on him, shy little house spiders climbed down walls until they were face-to-face in conversation with him, wild doves allowed him to pick them up and cradle them in his hands before gently putting them back down again. Dogs who barked, lunged, and bit at every other vet bared their teeth in goofy smiles at Dr. Frank. Cats he'd never met before rubbed their foreheads hard against his own and tapped their paws against his cheeks, their claws politely tucked away.

Children such as his own granddaughter tended to run up to his side and slip their hands into his. His daughters had done that, too, when they were little, but now he couldn't recall the last time he'd held their hands. Adults of the human species were a puzzle to him, mysteries to which he knew he hadn't a clue. His wife, Lorraine, was long dead, so he couldn't ask her how to reach his own girls again. It was when she died that he'd felt them slipping away; it was Lorraine, he then understood, who had long bridged the gap between them.

Dr. Frank observed the pert, upturned face of his granddaughter, whom he loved so much it made his heart swell and hurt, and felt sad at the thought of one day watching her, too, disappear into the mists of adulthood.

"Meow," she teased him.

He heard her and smiled.

It was how she called him out of the reveries into which he often sank these days, like an old dog in a patch of sunlight. His grandchild knew him well, he thought ruefully: If his phone barked instead of rang, he'd probably answer it more often.

"It's a murder story," he warned her. "Are you sure you want to hear it?"

"Oh, yes! As long as only people die. No animals, right?"

"I promise no animals die in this story."

"Okay, then."

He knew exactly how she felt and couldn't agree with her more.

"The victim was a man named Joseph Becker," he said,

settling back into the easy chair while she also settled herself more comfortably in the crook of his right arm, squeezed into the tiny space between him and the side of his chair. He heard her give a contented little sigh, and he felt like giving one just like it himself. "Joe Becker was a good-looking man in his thirties who was a partner in a small business that, um—" Dr. Couch thought, searching for a simple method of getting across to a ten-year-old the idea of a middleman "—that bought crops that farmers grew and sold them to big businesses. Most of the young men of our generation had gone off to fight in World War Two, but Joe Becker couldn't go, because he had flat feet."

Young Dr. Franklin Couch hadn't gone to war, either, not because he was a veterinarian, but because he was an only son who was already the sole support of a wife, two little daughters, and, to a lesser degree, his elderly parents. Often he wondered how his life would have been different if he'd served in the military—whether his life would have continued at all. There were times when he felt embarrassed among men of his own generation who had gone to Europe or the South Pacific or Asia. He suspected that feeling of embarrassment—which was partly guilt, but mostly just the sense of being an outsider—may have had something to do with why he had never made any close friends of his own age. It was almost as if he and other men his age didn't have much in common. They had the war. He had dogs and cats, birds and kids; and those were his social peers, it seemed.

On the whole, that was all right with him.

He'd never told anyone how he felt about himself and the war, not even Lorraine. She'd have told him he was silly, that it was a great accomplishment for a man to support a family and to serve his community, as he had done. But her words wouldn't have changed his feelings, he knew. And so there had never been any point in telling her.

"Meow?" said his granddaughter.

"Oh, yes. Joe Becker. Well, the unfortunate young man was found one Sunday in the autumn of nineteen forty-four, bashed in the head with a frying pan in his kitchen in his apartment. I knew Becker, you see, and I also knew all of the people who were considered suspects in his murder. Or at least I knew their pets. Becker, for instance, had a lovely little Siamese named Annie."

"Is that the cat you worried about, Grandpa?"

"That's the cat. But there were also all of the suspects and their animals. Some of the suspects had access but no opportunity, and some of them had opportunity but no motive, and—"

"What's a motive, Grandpa?"

He realized he was going to have to slow down and tell the story in a simple, logical fashion so the child could follow him. "A motive, Frankie, is a stupid reason for doing a bad thing."

"Like what?"

"Like the ex-wife, who wished Becker was dead so she could sell the apartment building they both still owned together, the one where they were both residing in separate units at the time that he was killed. The ex-wife, Mary Becker, was in apartment One-A, and Becker himself was in Two-B."

"Was she pretty?"

"Who? Mrs. Becker? I don't recall, but she had the ugliest old marmalade tom you ever saw. Name of JamPot. I certainly remember that. I'm sure he hated it; I would. JamPot! Some people have no sense of propriety or dignity when it comes to naming their animals! Poor JamPot. I don't think that cat ever won a single fight he was in, to judge by the number of times she'd had to bring him round to me to get him fixed up and stitched. He probably should have been neutered, although that might not have solved his problem. I've seen plenty of neutered toms'd take Mike Tyson out in two rounds. No, I suspect JamPot just had bad timing—always throwing his punches late, so to speak. He used to take a swipe at me when I treated him, but I always got my hand away in time. Poor timing, that was JamPot's problem.

"Anyway, the trouble with his owner as a suspect was that she had motive and access, but she apparently didn't have opportunity. The ex-Mrs. Becker claimed she was in Chicago visiting her mother at the time that her former husband was killed. From the police point of view, Mary Becker had bad timing, just like her cat."

"You always say people are like their animals."

"Do I always say that?"

"About once a day that I know of." She grinned up at him, her neck cocked as if she were looking up at the sun. "You probably say it other times when I'm not around."

He laughed, utterly delighted to be teased.

Adults, he knew, were rather intimidated by him, by his size, his age, his reputation. They tended to treat him with a reserve and respect he supposed they thought he deserved. On the whole, he much preferred to be teased.

"So, Grandpa, what's access? What's opportunity?"

Her grandfather was amused and pleased that he didn't have to explain *neutered* to her, but he did have to explain the legal parlance of a homicide investigation. You could tell she hung around vets and not lawyers! Good child! He quirked a bushy silver eyebrow at her and pretended to look stern.

"Access is being able to pull up a chair to the bookcase so you can reach my private collection of Hershey's Kisses with Almonds!"

13

He observed her eyes get large and her face grow pink.

"Opportunity is when you're in my office alone and I'm in the bathroom with the door closed!"

He watched her scrunch up her face so tight that her eyes shut.

"And motive is . . ." He waited for her eyes to open, and then he smiled at her. "Well, in the case of Hershey's Kisses, it's *not* a stupid and bad reason; it's a perfectly understandable and intelligent one, which is a wish for a taste of chocolate."

"I didn't take any pieces of candy!"

"When?"

"When what?"

"When didn't you take any?"

She thought about that, examined the twinkle in his eyes, and said judiciously, "Almost never."

Her grandfather guffawed, enormously impressed at how sharp she was. "That's a good one, Frankie!" He chuckled. "You almost never didn't take any!"

"Grandpa?"

"Yes?"

"I don't really like almonds."

"Then they will never darken my candy bowl again. But listen, child, you could break your neck climbing up on that chair." She was just like her miniature dachshund, he thought with pride, always aiming for things that were way above her head. "I'll put the bowl on a lower shelf. Now, do you want to hear about any of the other suspects in my little murder mystery?"

"I do! Especially the parts about their pets that you knew. And especially the part where you were worried about Mr. Becker's cat. Annie. The Siamese."

"Well, here's what happened," he began again happily.

"You know about the victim now?"

"Joe Becker," the child recited. "Bashed. Frying pan."

"Where?"

"Kitchen of where he lived. Um." She thought hard. "Apartment Two-A."

"No, Two-B. Remember, his ex-wife lived in One-A."

"Wait, wait!" commanded the child, excitedly. "Let me say it! Her name was Sherry, and she had a big marmalade tom named JamPot who never won any fights, and she couldn't have done it, because she was . . . someplace else."

"Her name was Mary," he corrected, gently, fully sympathetic to the fact that it was easier to recall the names of animals than people. "And it was Chicago. But you got everything else right. And what might have been her reason for wanting him dead?"

"She wanted his apartment?"

"She wanted to own the whole building so she could sell it."

Frankie lifted a delicate brown eyebrow. "Greedy pig."

"People often are, unfortunately. Now let me tell you about the other suspects in the murder."

"And their motives, opportunities, and excess."

"Access, although you do have a point there." He laughed. "Excess! Yes indeed, you would certainly find that was true in almost any murder case, I suspect. There would be an excess of something, wouldn't there, whether it was greed, or fear, or whatever."

"Other suspects," she reminded him.

"Yes. Well, there was Nancy Okawa, for instance, who had a nervous, skinny little white tomcat. She had access because she was Becker's girlfriend and so she had a key to his apartment, and she had opportunity, because she was in and out of the apartment all the time, but she didn't have any apparent motive."

15

"Like wanting chocolate," Frankie commented.

"Exactly. Apparently there wasn't anything the equivalent of chocolate that Nancy Okawa wanted that would require the death of her boyfriend, Joe Becker. She said she loved him madly. She appeared to be grief-stricken."

"What was her cat's name, Grandpa?"

"Lightning."

Frankie reacted disdainfully. "Sounds like a horse's name to me."

"I know, but it was perfect, because he was full of electricity."

The child laughed, and Dr. Couch knew she was picturing in her agile, imaginative mind a skinny white cat that was constantly jumping and racing about.

"You're too young to know this," her grandfather continued, "but there is a clue to the victim's character in the name of his girlfriend. Can you possibly guess what it is?"

Frankie frowned in heavy thought, and repeated to herself several times in a low voice, "Nancy Okawa, Nancy Okawa, Nancy Okawa." Suddenly she brightened. "Was she, like, Japanese? Is that the clue?"

"Very good! Nancy wasn't 'like' Japanese; she was a child of Japanese parents who had immigrated to this country soon after she was born. These days people feel free to fall in love with anybody they want to, but in those days there was a lot of prejudice when a white person went around with a person of a different race, not to mention the fact that this country was at war with Japan, so a lot of people looked on Nancy Okawa as the enemy. She had even lived in a concentration camp with her parents for a time in California. Now what does this suggest to you about the character of our victim, Joseph Becker?"

"He didn't care what anybody thought?" Frankie guessed.

"Brilliant child. That is exactly right, although it wasn't

precisely the same thing as courage or even tolerance. Becker was just an aggressive, imperious sort of fellow who didn't let anybody or anything stand in the way of what he wanted, not other people's prejudices, not even a war."

"He sounds like a Siamese."

"Some Siamese, you're right. But his lovely Annie was elegantly imperious, like a benevolent queen, while he had always struck me as being a bit of a thug. I should tell you that Annie was a housecat, Frankie. Becker never, never, never allowed her to go outside or anywhere else, for that matter, because he wanted to breed her and make money from her litters."

Again the delicate eyebrow lifted. "Greedy pig."

"There's a lot of that to go around in this story," her grandfather admitted. "Perhaps I should tell you how I became involved."

"Yes!"

"It was simple, really. I received a summons from the man who was our police chief at the time. He sent one of his fellows over to fetch me, because Annie had crawled up on top of Joe Becker's shower-curtain pole, and she was hissing at all of the police officers and she wouldn't come down. He just wanted me to come get her and take her away from the scene of the murder."

"So you saw it!" The child's light brown eyes were huge with awe.

"Blood and all," her grandfather agreed.

They both nodded in mutual satisfaction.

"I saw Becker's body in the kitchen," the old man told her. "And got a good look around the whole apartment, because Annie gave me quite a little chase!"

They smiled, then laughed together, he at the memory of his undignified pursuit of the furious feline and she at the idea of her big old grandfather racing around after a cat.

"I brought her home with me," he continued. "And I examined her, because she had a little blood on her, and that's when I discovered she was—"

But the eager, curious child interrupted him. "What'd you see in Mr. Becker's apartment? Was it full of cops? Did you find any clues? Was his girlfriend there?"

"No, but his upstairs neighbor was, because he always looked after Annie whenever Joe Becker was traveling on business. It was the neighbor who called the police to tell them he'd found the body. His name was Alastair Reynolds, and he owned a local bakery."

She wasn't interested in that. "Did he have a pet?"

"Everybody in this story had a pet." Her grandfather smiled. "Alastair Reynolds, the baker, had a big, sweet-natured tom named, appropriately enough, Sugar. Sugar was one of my favorite patients. He was a handsome fellow, all soft and shiny black except for three white paws. He looked as if he had stepped in the flour when his owner was baking bread."

Frankie pressed her hands against her grandfather's upper right arm and worked her fingers up and down as if she were a baker kneading bread or a cat kneading his arm. If he could have purred, he would have at that perfect moment in his long life.

"I haven't told you about the partner yet, have I?"

"Whose partner? Mr. Becker's? Tell me, tell me."

"Yes, Joe Becker's partner in the food distribution business was a big blond fellow who never smiled, by the name of Quentin Dees. He didn't have any cats or even a wife but he did have three Doberman pinschers that he kept locked up behind a high fence at his house. I do believe they were the most sinister dogs I ever met, because they prowled constantly but never made a sound. Instead of barking at strangers, those three dogs would come together in a trio at the fence line and bare their teeth at you. It was worth your life to step onto that property unannounced."

Frankie shivered pleasurably in the crook of his arm and whispered, "What did he call them?"

"He didn't give them names. He would just call *Dog* in a sharp, high voice, and they all three would obey him instantly."

"I don't like that man, Grandpa!"

"No reason you should, Frankie."

The child suddenly looked excited. "I'll bet he killed Mr. Becker, didn't he?"

"Well, now wait," he cautioned. "Let's not rush to any conclusions. You may be right, or you may not. Hop up and get us a handful of Hershey's Kisses, and we'll examine the evidence. They're not on the upper shelf anymore, Frankie; they're on top of my desk. In case you hadn't noticed."

She grinned and scooted down from his lap.

When she hopped back up, she had a double handful of candy to pour into his own cupped hands. Fastidiously, Frankie picked the plain Hersheys without nuts out of the pile he patiently held for her. Only when she was finished did he shift the remaining sweets to his left palm so that he could open the silver wrappings with his right hand. For a few contented moments, grandfather and grandchild rustled paper and chewed chocolate together. "When you're older," he observed, "you'll like the almond ones better."

"Yuk."

They allowed the foil and the little white streamers to drift to the carpet below them.

"I am thinking," Dr. Frank said, as with a bare finger he dabbed a peck of chocolate off a corner of her mouth, "that there may be no way you can guess the truth about this story, because you don't have the memories of wartime that adults have. There is certain crucial information that you're missing—at least one clue that a grownup might be able to surmise just from what I have told you so far—but if I tell you what it is, you'll guess the truth immediately." He surreptitiously wiped his brown fingertip on the underside of the upholstered arm of the chair. "What should I do, Frankie, tell you or not tell you?"

"Don't tell me! Let me guess!"

"All right." He wrinkled his forehead in thought, and when he did, his granddaughter kissed the side of his face. As if her kiss had given him inspiration, he suddenly smiled brightly and said, "I know. There's another way to allow you to figure out the truth, and you don't even have to be eighty years old to do it. What I started to tell you earlier was that when I brought Annie home with me, I examined her because she had a little blood on her."

"Was she hurt?"

Her grandfather realized that although he had promised her no animals would die in the story, he had neglected to guarantee that none of them would be harmed at all.

"No, no," he assured her, quickly. "It was her owner's blood, not hers. No, when I examined her I discovered that what Annie was, was pregnant."

"But he never let her out of the apartment!"

Her grandfather gave her a meaningful stare. "Exactly!"

"Is that the clue?" she asked, excitedly.

He merely smiled and said nothing to assist her.

The child thought and thought, but she was only ten years old, and finally she cried out in frustration, "I don't get it! How can I tell who killed Mr. Becker from just knowing that Annie was going to have kittens?"

Dr. Frank hugged and patted her. "You'll get it. I'll tell you a bit more of the story, and then you'll figure out why that clue is so important."

"Okay," she said a little sulkily.

Her grandfather thought for a moment about how to tell the remainder of it so that it would be impossible for her to guess wrong. "At first," he continued, "the police were sure the girlfriend did it, probably just because she was of Japanese ancestry. But even they had to admit she didn't seem to have any motive for killing him, and she was too short to have been able to reach up and clobber him so effectively with the frying pan."

"He could have been bending over," Frankie pointed out.

"Perhaps they didn't think of that," her grandfather said, keeping his expression quite serious.

The child looked once again satisfied with her own intelligence.

"Then, when they couldn't pin it on her, they decided the wife did it, because she did have a motive . . ."

"But no opportunity!" Frankie crowed.

"That's right."

"I told you the mean partner did it—I told you he did it!"

"Well, Frankie, that is very astute character analysis on your part, because the police discovered that Joe Becker and Quentin Dees had also been partners in an illegal business called the black market. During wartime, you see, certain goods were what was called rationed, which meant that the most important substances, like flour and sugar and butter and rubber and nylon, were put aside for the war effort, leaving only a little for the rest of us to share for domestic purposes on the home front." He gazed into her eyes, which was a little like looking backwards through time into a photograph

21

of his own eyes when he was a boy. "Do you understand what
I just said?"

"Do I *have* to understand it?" she asked candidly.

Her grandfather laughed. "No, not really. I'll just say one
more thing about it, which is that these men were diverting
some of the goods they bought from farmers and selling those
goods illegally to private individuals instead of to the government."

"Is that why his partner killed him?"

"The police arrested his partner, Quentin Dees, after they
discovered the illegal business the two men had been con-
ducting. Dees admitted that Joe Becker had decided to get
out of the business, because it was getting too dangerous and
he was afraid of getting caught. They accused Quentin Dees
of killing him to prevent him from ever telling anybody what
they had been doing."

"That was his . . . motive?"

Dr. Frank nodded.

"Did he have"—carefully she pronounced it—"access?"

"And opportunity? Yes, indeed. He had a key to the apartment, and he was even seen leaving there the morning that
Becker was killed. The neighbor reported hearing the two
men yelling at each other and then seeing Dees leave by the
front door."

"That was dumb."

"For a murderer, yes."

"Is that the end of the story?" She didn't look entirely satisfied, her grandfather noticed. He certainly didn't want to
disappoint her.

"Not exactly," he said. "There is one more loose end we
have to tie up. Can you think what it is?"

He could almost see all the many details of the story he
had told her going rapidly through her bright mind as she re-

viewed them, searching for the loose end. He could even tell when, a second before she announced it, she found it.

"Annie!" she shouted triumphantly. "Her kittens!"

"One kitten," the old vet said. "Annie only had one kitten in that first litter. Can you imagine what it looked like, Frankie?"

"A Siamese, of course."

"No, it didn't look very much like a Siamese."

Suddenly, the child's eyes grew wide and her mouth dropped open. "Oh, my gosh! What did it look like, Grandpa, what did it look like?"

"What *could* it look like, Frankie?"

"Oh, gosh, oh, gosh, let me remember all the cats!" She was bouncing up and down on his lap, so excited she couldn't stay still. "There was the skinny little white tom that Mr. Becker's girlfriend owned, and there was the pretty black tom with white paws that the upstairs neighbor owned, and there was the ugly old marmalade tom that the ex-wife owned. Grandpa! The partner owned dogs! He didn't kill Mr. Becker! He didn't kill Mr. Becker, did he?!"

"No, Frankie, he didn't."

"Whichever tomcat that Annie's kitten looked like, it was that cat's owner that killed him, wasn't it?"

"Yes, it was, Frankie."

"Don't tell me, don't tell me!"

For a few long moments, the child sat deep in thought.

When she finally looked up at him, she looked much calmer, even sure of herself. "JamPot's owner was in Chicago, so she didn't do it. Lightning's owner really loved Mr. Becker, and she didn't have any reason to kill him, so she didn't do it. Grandpa, was the baby kitty black with three white paws?"

Solemnly, he nodded. "Just as if he had stepped in flour."

"It was the neighbor," Frankie announced, with equal solemnity. Then she looked frustrated again. "But why did he do it? He had opportunity—because he was there that Sunday. And he had access, I guess—because he must have had a key if he was taking care of Annie when Mr. Becker traveled. But what was his motive, Grandpa?"

He smiled at her. "That's the part you'd have to be a grownup to have guessed. Remember I said he was a local baker, Frankie? What do bakers need to do their job? Things like flour, butter, and sugar, all of which were rationed and difficult for small bakers to get in the quantities they needed in order to keep their businesses going. The upstairs neighbor was a very ambitious man who wanted his little bakery to *grow,* not merely keep going. He'd been purchasing black-market goods from Mr. Becker, and when Becker announced he couldn't do that anymore, he flew into a rage and grabbed the frying pan and beat him with it."

"Oh," said Frankie, nodding wisely.

"As for the cats," her grandfather concluded, "as you may imagine, the baker wasn't a very ethical person. He knew how persnickety Mr. Becker was about Annie, but he didn't care. So when Mr. Becker was out of town, sometimes he left the doors open, and his own sweet black tomcat followed him inside. And that's how it happened."

"But Grandpa, you always say that people are like their cats. If Sugar was really so sweet, how could her owner be such a bad man?"

He smiled at her. "The baker had a very nice wife."

"So Sugar the boy cat fell in love with Annie the girl cat, and they had a baby kitty named—?"

"Cupcake."

"Did they get married?"

"No, dear, they had Cupcake out of wedlock."

A noise at the doorway made both of them look around.

There stood Frankie's mother, who was Dr. Frank's youngest daughter, looking in at them. "Dad," she said, "do you think a story like that is appropriate for a child her age?"

"Oh, dear, I don't know. I'm sorry! Do you think . . ."

"Let's wait until she's a little older, shall we?"

"Oh, well, yes, if you think so . . ."

"Yes," his daughter continued, "we can wait awhile longer for the birds and the bees."

Her father thought: *Birds and bees? That was what she objected to?* As he lifted Frankie off his lap so she could run to her mother, he happily thought: *Great! If that's all the problem is, next time I'll tell Frankie about the dog who caught a serial murderer!*

At the doorway, the child turned around to ask one last question. "What happened to Sugar and Annie and Cupcake, Grandpa?"

"Sugar stayed with the baker's nice wife," he told her. "And I gave Annie and Cupcake to a kind family who lived in the country. I drove them both out together on Arbor Day of that year, and it was wonderful to get to see Annie run and play outside for once in her life. I even got to see her climb a tree, as if she were celebrating her own personal, very first Arbor Day."

"Oh, Dad," said his daughter, laughing.

But his granddaughter nodded, as if she understood everything perfectly. They smiled at each other as her mother gently pulled her from the room. After a moment of sitting still and listening to their departure, Dr. Frank bent over to begin to pick up the silver foil and white paper streamers that littered the carpet at his feet.

25

The Cairo Cat Caper

Peter Schweighofer

Duncan Barstowe was quickly tiring of Mrs. Strasser's attentive chattering when he spotted the messenger. A young Arab lad, head swathed in a turban, fought his way through the carriage drivers, fruit-sellers, camel masters, and beggars who cluttered the street in front of Shepheard's Hotel. He spotted Barstowe having breakfast on the hotel verandah. The boy's eyes appealed to the old gentleman as if he'd try evading the waif, but Duncan simply set the *Daily Mail* on the table and calmly awaited his arrival.

Cavendish looked up from her bowl of milk beside Barstowe's chair to glare at Mrs. Strasser. Her incessant babbling clearly annoyed him, too. The black cat rolled her eyes and returned to her milk.

"I was surprised not to see your husband at the opera last night," Barstowe replied. "Nor at Mrs. Clayton's soiree at the Hotel Continental."

"Oh, Professor Strasser was lost mingling in the opera crowd," she replied. "He so adores *Aida*. But he retired early. He spends his nights studying his papyrus scrolls and keeping extensive notes from our daily excursions."

"And ignores the affections of so dutiful and fair a wife? He can't even join you for breakfast?" Barstowe kept his eyes on the young messenger, now pleading politely with the two doormen who kept the unruly street rabble from bothering Shepheards' guests. Each guard rested his meaty hands on pistols thrust through a colorful sash. One peered over at Barstowe, who slightly nodded his head. The doormen allowed the boy to pass.

"The Professor's responsibilities for the university require constant attention," Mrs. Strasser explained.

"Ah, yes, he's teaching at the University of Berlin. How is Professor Lepsius these days? Did your husband accompany him to Egypt in 1845 during the last Prussian expedition?"

"Goodness, no, he was just a little boy then, though news of Lepsius' discoveries inspired his interest in archaeology. Actually, the Professor was hoping you'd accompany me to view the pyramids today," she chimed, placing a gentle hand on Barstowe's arm. "We can hire camels to take us to Gizeh."

"Goodness, Mrs. Strasser, I haven't all day to spend sightseeing. In fact, I believe a situation requiring my immediate attention approaches."

The Arab boy arrived and bowed deeply to Barstowe. He jumped back in fright when he noticed Cavendish sitting at his feet. The cat looked like a haunting statue from ancient times, propped up on her haunches like the goddess Bastet appreciating this mortal's adoration. The messenger muttered some Mohammedan incantation against efreets before continuing. "*Salaam aleikum,* Barstowe Bey," he said, bowing deeply again, though with a wary eye on Cavendish. "I bring a message from Mariette Bey." He produced a folded paper slip from his sash and handed it reverently to Barstowe.

Cavendish hopped onto the table, reveling coyly at Mrs. Strasser's discomfort with the intrusion into her breakfast-table realm. Barstowe held the note far enough away so the cat could read it, too, though still close enough that Mrs.

Strasser could not. He stroked his whitened goatee as he scanned the message:

Dear Monsieur B—

Your reputation for explaining mysterious occurrences and solving unspeakable crimes precedes you. I humbly request your assistance in a most urgent matter. Last night someone broke into the museum at Boulak and stole several valuable pieces of New Empire jewelry. The guards are at a loss to explain the incident. Surely your keen intellect and powers of deduction can solve this baffling occurrence and recover the lost pieces.

Your humble servant,
A. Mariette

"What's happened?" Mrs. Strasser pestered.

Barstowe and Cavendish looked up at her over the note. "I'm afraid there's been some trouble at the museum," the gentleman explained. The cat simply peered at Mrs. Strasser as if the matter were none of her business. Barstowe folded the note and slipped it into his frock coat pocket. He caught a hotel servant's attention: "Would you kindly fetch my walking stick and top hat, lad." Barstowe snapped his fingers and a gold sovereign appeared in his hand. He presented it to the Arab messenger. "My good boy, please summon a hansom cab. I must leave for the Boulak Museum at once."

"Surely you can't let such a trivial affair interfere with our delightful breakfast and our plans to view the pyramids and sphinx," Mrs. Strasser pleaded, earning another disinterested glance from Cavendish.

"Indeed, Mrs. Strasser, it is not my responsibility but the Professor's to look after your daily tourist amusements. Please express my apologies to him for abandoning you to the hotel's fine hospitality and courteous staff."

Barstowe strode to the Boulak Museum's entrance as if it weren't a warehouse filled with antiquities but a pharaoh's palace. Despite the top hat somewhat too tall for his own stature, he still stood shorter than the two Egyptian soldiers in blue uniforms and red fez. "The museum is closed today," they announced.

Cavendish, scampering along at Barstowe's feet, stopped to glare at the guards. Barstowe's hands grasped the brass knob atop his walking stick and planted the stout wood before him. "Mons. Mariette summoned me," he explained. "I am Duncan Barstowe."

The soldiers glared suspiciously at Cavendish, then parted and opened the museum doors. The interior was arranged as best it could as a museum, but still held the air of a warehouse crammed with ancient treasures. Statues of pharaohs, sphinxes and gods milled about. Upright and flat wood-and-glass cases crammed against each other. Crowds of mummies and their sarcophagi lounged against a wall. Barstowe found August Mariette towering over two sarcophagi which had fallen over, smashing two glass cases on two adjacent tables. Two soldiers stood rigidly, absorbing the brunt of Mariette's tirade about the robbery.

One of the museum guards noticed their visitor, interrupting Mariette's outburst to divert his attention to the gentleman and his cat. Barstowe presented his card, which one solider relayed to Mariette. The man's stormy countenance cleared. "Ah, Monsieur Barstowe," he said, removing his fez. "I'm glad you answered our plea for aid. I am Auguste Mariette, Director of Egyptian Monuments and curator of this modest museum."

"The pleasure is mine, Mons. Mariette." Barstowe swept

the hat from his head and bowed deeply. "My belated condolences on your daughter's passing. And sincere congratulations on your citation for scholarship from the *Académie des Inscriptions.*"

Mariette allowed a grim smile to dawn amidst his beard. "Life's small achievements are rarely won without sacrifice and sorrow," he noted solemnly. "And now thieves plague our humble museum. I'm a scholar of ancient Egypt, Monseiur—I don't understand the ways of thieves nor the means by which investigators such as yourself uncover and solve their crimes."

Cavendish stepped from behind Barstowe and wrapped herself around Mariette's legs. "This must be your infamous feline companion." He chuckled to himself when the cat began purring. The Egyptian guards kept their distance.

"Yes, Cavendish and I must begin our investigations at once," Barstowe announced. "Have a look around, won't you my friend?" Mariette shot Barstowe an odd glance, thinking the old gentleman addressed him. Cavendish scampered off toward mountains of wooden packing crates near an office door. "Now, Monsieur, please show me the crime scene and tell me what the thieves stole."

Mariette directed them to the smashed cases. The soldiers followed warily. "Here," he said. "Someone toppled these sarcophagi onto the glass cases and tables, shattering everything. These vitrines held priceless New Empire jewelry. Small pieces, but of immeasurable value."

Barstowe knelt down and poked the debris with his walking stick. He found several gold rings and amulets among the splintered wood, shattered glass and wrinkled velvet. "Apparently the thieves didn't take all the jewelry from these cases," he noted. "Either they didn't want them, or they couldn't take them."

Mariette glanced at the remaining pieces. "They're just as valuable as those taken."

"Did your guards notice anything?" Barstowe asked, prodding a bit of grayish powder with his finger. "Interrupt the robbery-in-progress, perhaps, or catch the villains fleeing the premises?"

"No, they are assigned to patrol outside while the building is locked tight," Mariette replied. He nodded to one of the guards accompanying them. "Though Abdullah here, their overseer, discovered the robbery this morning. He suspects his men were dozing."

Barstowe rose, rubbing the gray dust between his fingers, then sniffing it cautiously. "Abdullah, please question your soldiers, both those on duty last night and those posted here while the museum is open."

"Certainly, *effendi*," he replied with a curt bow, then trotted off with his assistant to round up the guards.

Cavendish reappeared, pawing Barstowe's boot. With Mariette in tow he followed the cat to the crates she'd examined. "What's in these boxes, and who's looked in them recently?"

Mariette casually removed one lid and set it aside. "Storage mostly. Relics not important enough to display in our limited space. The Viceroy commissioned a new museum, still under construction, where most of these antiquities will eventually find new homes."

Cavendish yowled at one box with the lid slightly ajar. Though the cat could have slipped in through the hole, he clearly had no desire to do so. Barstowe removed the lid and peered inside while Mariette droned on. "Few people examine the relics in these crates. Mostly scholars from the Continent. Tourists have little interest in these artifacts, though we will eventually examine and catalog each. They're

31

open, of course, if you'd like to examine them," he added belatedly, the stormy expression clouding his face again.

"You kept mummies in this particular crate," Barstowe declared.

"Yes, clearly you can see that box is packed with animal mummies . . ." Mariette stopped when Barstowe withdrew a shredded mummy shroud about a foot long. "My heavens, someone's desecrated that cat mummy."

"Tore the wrappings to pieces," Barstowe said, opening the ripped bandages. They crinkled like ancient, dried newspaper. "And stole the mummy." He'd pried the shroud apart, revealing the cavity which once held a desiccated cat. Cavendish batted the wrappings with her paw. Barstowe drew several more empty mummy husks from the crate. Some smiled back with bemused cat faces painted on them, now split in two cross-eyed halves by whoever ripped them open.

"Who would steal cat mummies but leave the wrappings behind?" Mariette asked.

Barstowe almost brushed the dust from his hands, then halted abruptly. He sniffed his hands, then ground the fine gray powder between his fingers. "Mummy dust. Believed to have certain medicinal qualities in earlier, less enlightened times. I found bits of it within the display case wreckage, too."

Everyone turned toward a startled cry from Mariette's office. "I did nothing wrong, merely overlooked something, that's all." Apparently Abdullah managed to pry a confession from one of his guards. He and another soldier dragged the unfortunate man from the office and presented him before Mariette.

"Musmar claims he overlooked one of the window shutters, which he left unlocked and ajar last night," Abdullah proclaimed. "Would you like us to beat him until he tells the entire truth?"

"Come now, that's quite unnecessary," Barstowe replied.

Cavendish appeared and nuzzled the guard's legs. He screamed and struggled against the soldiers holding his arms. "Keep it away! It curses me with its eyes! Save me, Mariette Bey, from this awful efreet. I'll tell everything. Please . . ."

"Enough, Cavendish." The cat sauntered back to Barstowe for a gentle pat on the head. He opened his palm for her to sniff, then she scurried off.

"Now, Musmar, what happened?" Mariette growled.

"A man approached me as I left the night before last," Musmar stammered. "He offered me many gold sovereigns if I would leave one window shutter unlocked and ajar before I left last night."

"What did the fiend look like?" Mariette pressed.

"It was dark, but I saw he wore Westerner's clothes, and a top hat."

Mariette snorted. "You've just described every European gentleman in Cairo!"

Cavendish's yowling summoned everyone's attention to a high, narrow window near a pharaoh's statue. The tall shutter swung inward slightly, unlocked. Cavendish prodded with her paws, then wriggled easily through the narrow opening.

Barstowe stepped up to examine the window ledge more closely. He probed with his fingers, finally removing a torn piece of mummy shroud. Mariette stepped back in awe. "And there's gray mummy dust everywhere," Barstowe said. "There are little dabbings of it all over this sculpture—in the shape of cat paws."

Mariette shook his head. "Certainly you're not suggesting . . ."

"Summon a carriage, my friend," Barstowe commanded, stepping lightly down from the statue. "We're off to Shepheard's Hotel."

"Goodness, man, this is no time for a fancy lunch and tea with socialites!"

"We'll have lunch, certainly . . . after I've recovered your stolen artifacts. I'll warn you, though, my explanation defies any logic you or the police wish to apply."

One of Shepheards' imposing doormen led them to the Strassers' room. Cavendish warily eyed the two calicoes and a tabby pawing at the door. Barstowe and Mariette heard more cats wailing through an open window inside the chambers.

"Quick, shut that trunk and call the porter. We can just make it to the railway station and catch the noon train." The muffled words came from within, along with the banging and clattering of hurried packing.

Barstowe pointed his walking stick's brass knob at the cats. *"Hepre per, miu!"* he commanded. The felines scampered down the hotel corridor and around a corner. Cavendish twitched but held her ground. Barstowe rapped the door with his cane.

Mrs. Strasser answered, opening the door a crack. "Why Mister Cavendish, what a pleasant surprise . . ."

With his stick Barstowe effortlessly swung the door wide, freeing it from the woman's feeble grasp. Disorder reigned in the room beyond. Cargo trunks crowded the chambers, each open and overflowing with clothes and traveling articles. Professor Strasser jammed papers into his valise. While his wife blushed, his own face was haggard from lack of sleep.

"I believe you possess some items from Mons. Mariette's museum," Barstowe announced.

Professor Strasser dropped the valise to the writing desk.

Anger filtered through his weary eyes.

"Your feline accomplices left quite an assortment of clues at the museum, though only I could stretch the bounds of logic to interpret them," Barstowe said, striding into the chambers. He peered out the window, waved his walking stick, shouted *"Hepre per, miu!"* again, and the cats weeping in the courtyard below dispersed. "Surely, Professor, you could not expect cats to go long without sustenance. And these are like any other, from Egypt's New Empire to those in Queen Victoria's empire—they wish their master to feed them some milk and offer a bit of affection, as their moods warrant."

Cavendish scampered in after Mariette and the doorman, leaping onto the table and batting through the Professor's papers. "Thus, my friends, Professor Strasser's instruments of thievery inadvertently revealed his crime through their very nature." Cavendish stared disapprovingly at Barstowe as if she were above it all, then returned to pawing the Professor's notes. Several documents floated to the floor, each covered in copied hieroglyphics. Barstowe retrieved them and glanced at the texts. "Ancient magic," he noted. "How innovative. I'll dispose of these. As for your thievery, I'm sure Mons. Mariette would kindly overlook your transgressions, as long as you surrender the jewelry and leave Egypt at once . . . as, apparently, you were preparing to do anyway."

A puzzled expression dispelled the anger growing on Mariette's face. "Why, of course, anything to return such valuable pieces to the museum."

Mrs. Strasser blushed again, then turned to dig through a traveling trunk. She produced a velvet drawstring bag, which she presented to Mariette. He opened it, a look of marvel and delight dawning on his countenance.

"If you're to catch the midday train to Alexandria, I suggest you depart with haste," Barstowe said. "Kindly leave any antiquities you picked up during your shopping excursions to the bazaar, if you please. We'll let Mon. Mariette examine them to determine their authenticity."

The Professor grabbed his valise and shuffled out the door, but his wife lingered. Barstowe removed his top hat and bowed slightly. "My dear, it was perfectly apparent this morning's quaint breakfast conversation and exhortation to accompany you to the pyramids was little more than a ploy to make me unavailable to investigate Mons. Mariette's dilemma—at least until you left on the evening train to Alexandria. Thank you, it was quite amusing in retrospect, but your attentions were quite unwarranted."

Mrs. Strasser spun on her heel and stalked down the hotel corridor behind her husband. Cavendish looked up from toying with an inkpot to glare after the woman. Barstowe turned to the doorman. "Have their baggage delivered to Alexandria once you've thoroughly examined it with Mons. Mariette."

"But the cats," Mariette exclaimed, still missing one puzzle piece for himself. "You don't really believe they were the same one's contained within the mummy shrouds?"

"Oh, certainly not, my friend," Barstowe with a mischievous grin. "Sheer coincidence, I assure you. You don't really think sorcerers walk this earth raising cat mummies from the dead and performing other feats of stage magic?"

"Well, I . . . I suppose not."

"Exactly. Come along, Cavendish; time for lunch. And perhaps later we shall visit the howling dervishes."

The cat peered at Barstowe with a tolerant expression.

"Perhaps not," the gentleman added.

Sax and the Single Cat

Carole Nelson Douglas

The day I get the call, I am lounging on Miss Temple Barr's patio at the Circle Ritz condominiums in Las Vegas, trying to soak up what little January sunshine deigns to shed some pallid photosynthesis on my roommate's potted oleanders.

Next thing I know, some strange Tom in a marmalade-striped T-shirt is over the marble-faced wall and in my own face.

It is not hard to catch Midnight Louie napping these days, but I am on my feet and bristling the hair on my muscular nineteen-pound-plus frame before you can say "Muhammad Ali." My butterfly-dancing days may be on hold, but I still carry a full set of bee-stingers on every extremity.

Calm down, the intruder advises in a throaty tone I do not like. He is only a messenger, he tells me next; Ingram wants to see me.

This I take exception to. Ingram is one of my local sources, and usually the sock is on the other foot: I want to see Ingram. When I do, I trot up to the Thrill 'n' Quill bookstore on Charleston to accomplish this dubious pleasure in person.

I look over my yellow-coated visitor and ask, "Since when has Ingram used Western Union?"

Since, says the dude with a snarl, he has a message for me from Kitty Kong. The intruder then leaps back from whence he came—Gehenna, I hope, but the city pound will do—and is as gone as a catnip dream.

A shiver plays arpeggios on my spine, which does nothing to restore my ruffled body hair.

This Kitty Kong is nobody to mess with, having an ancestry that predates saber-toothed tigers, who are really nothing to mess with. They would make Siegfried and Roy's menagerie at the Mirage Hotel look like animated powder-room rugs.

Though the designated titleholder changes, there is always a Kitty Kong. Long ago and far away, in Europe in pre-New World days, this character was known as the King of Cats, but modern times have caught up even with such a venerable institution. Nowadays Kitty Kong can as easily be a she as a he, or even an it. Nobody knows who or what, but the word gets out.

Supposedly, a Kitty Kong rules on every continent, the seven-plus seas being the only deterrent to rapid communication. Even today, dudes and dolls of my ilk hate to get their feet wet. If the aforementioned saber-tooths had been as particular, they would have avoided a lot of tar pits, but these awesome types are legend and long gone. Only Midnight Louie remains to do the really tough jobs, and at least I resemble an escapee from a tar pit.

I follow my late visitor over the edge to the street two stories below and am soon padding the cold Las Vegas pavement. Nobody much notices me—except the occasional cooing female, whom I nimbly evade—which is the way I like it.

Ingram you cannot miss. He is usually to be found snoozing amongst the murder and mayhem displayed in the window of the Thrill 'n' Quill. Today is different. He is waiting on the stoop.

38

"You are late, Louie," he sniffs.

Such criticism coming from someone who never has to go anywhere but the vet's does not sit well. I give the rabies tags on his collar a warning tap, then ask for the straight poop.

"And vulgar," he comments, but out it comes. A problem of national significance to catkind has developed and Kitty Kong wants me in Washington to help.

No wonder Ingram is snottier than usual; he is jealous. But his long, languorous days give him plenty of time to keep up with current events.

I am not a political animal by nature, but even I have noticed that the new Democratic administration in Washington means the White House will be blessed with the first dude of my ilk in a long, long time, one Socks (somehow that name always makes my nose wrinkle like it had been stuffed in a dirty laundry basket). However, I am not so socially apathetic as to avoid a thrill of satisfaction that one of Our Own is back in power after a long period when the position of presidential pet had gone to the dogs.

This First Feline, as the press so nauseatingly tagged the poor dude, is not the first of his kind to pussyfoot around the national premises. I recall that a polytoed type named Slippers was FDR's house cat and the White House's most recent First Adolescent, Amy Carter, had a Siamese named Misty Malarky Ying Yang. Come to think of it, Socks is not such a bad moniker at that.

Anyway, Ingram says the inauguration is only two days away and a revolting development has occurred: The President's cat is missing; slipped out of the First Lady's Oldsmobile near the White House that very morning. We cannot have our national icon (Ingram uses phrases like that) going AWOL (he does not use expressions like that, but I do) at so elevated an occasion. The mission, should I choose to accept it (and there is nil choice when Kitty Kong calls): find this Socks character and get him back on the White House lawn doing his do-do where he is supposed to do it.

The reason Midnight Louie is regarded as a one-dude detection service is some modest fame I have in the missing-persons department. A while back I hit the papers for finding a dead body at the American Booksellers convention, but I also solved the kidnapping of a couple of corporate kitties named Baker and Taylor. Things like that get back to Kitty Kong.

You would be surprised to know how fast cats like us can communicate. Fax machines may be zippy, but MCI (Multiple Cat Intelligence) can cross the country in a flash through a secret network of telecats who happen to look innocent and wear a lot of fur. These telecats are rare, but you can bet that they are well looked out for. I have never met one myself, but then I have never met a First Cat, either, and it looks like I will be doing that shortly.

After I leave Ingram, I ponder how to get to Washington, D.C. I could walk (and hitch a few rides along the way), but that is a dangerous and time-consuming trek. I prefer the direct route when possible.

Do I know anyone invited to the shindig? Not likely. Miss Temple Barr and her associates are nice folk but neither high nor low enough to come to this particular party. I doubt any of the Fifty Faces of America hails from Las Vegas (though several million such faces pass through here every year). I would have had better odds with the other guy and his "Thousand Points of Light."

But *que será, será,* and by the time I look up my feet have done their duty and taken me just where I need to be: Earl E. Byrd's Reprise storefront, a haven for secondhand instruments of a musical nature and Earl E. himself.

If anyone from my neck of the wilderness is going to Washington, it will be Earl E., owing to his sideline. I scratch at the door until he opens it. Earl E. stocks a great supply of meaty tidbits, for good reason, and I am a regular.

Of course, when I visit Earl E., I have to put up with Nose E.

I do not quite know how to describe this individual, and I am seldom at a loss for words. Nose E. resembles the product of an ill-advised mating between a goat-hair rug and a permanent-wave machine of the old school. Imagine a white angora dust mop with a hyperactive hamster inside and a rakish red bow over one long, floppy ear. Say it tips the scale at four pounds, is purportedly male and canine. There you have Nose E., one of the primo dope-and-bomb-sniffing types in Las Vegas, even the U.S. You figure it.

Earl E. has a secret, and lucrative, sideline in playing with bands at celebrity dos all over the country. The lucrative part is that Nose E. goes along in some undercover cop's grip, ready to squeal on any activities of an illegal nature among the guests, including those so rude as to disrupt the doings with an incendiary device.

Dudes and dolls of my particular persuasion are barred from this cushy job for moral reasons. Our well-known weakness for a bit of nip now and then supposedly makes us unreliable.

Oh. Did I mention Earl E.'s instrument of choice? Tenor sax. Will Earl E. be at the inauguration? As sure as it rains cats and dogs (that *look* like dogs) in Arkansas.

Commercial airliners are not my favorite form of travel, but with Earl E., I and Nose E. get separate but equal cardboard boxes and a seat in first-class. (Actually, my box is bigger than Nose E.'s, since I outweigh this dust-mop dude almost five to one.)

Getting here is not hard—after I gnaw on the heavy cream parchment of Earl E.'s invitation for a few minutes he gets the idea and says, "What is happenin', Louie? You want to go to D.C. today with Nose E. and me and boogie?"

I look as adorable as a guy of my age and weight can stomach, and wait.

"All right. I am paying for an extra seat anyway for the sax and Nose E. A formerly homeless black cat like you should have a chance to see history made."

See it? I make it. But that is my little secret.

As per the usual, there is little room at the inn in D.C., but Earl E. has connections due to his vocations of music and marijuana sniffing. My carrier converts into a litter box for a few days in a motel room not too far from the Capitol with a king-size bed I much approve and promptly fall asleep on for the night, despite the company. I also plan to use most of my facilities outdoors, reconnoitering.

Naturally, Earl E. has no intentions of letting me out unchaperoned, though he takes that miserable Nose E. everywhere. Imagine a Hostess coconut cupcake sitting on some dude's elbow and squeaking every now and then. But there is not a hotel maid alive who can see past her ankles fast enough to contain Midnight Louie when he is doing a cha-cha between the door and a service cart.

I am a bit hazy on dates when denied access to the Daily Doormat—otherwise known as the morning paper—but I discover later that we arrived on the day before the inauguration.

Washington in January is snowless, but my horizon is an expanse of gray pavement and looming white monuments, so the effect is wintry despite a delicate dome of blue backdropping it all.

I stroll past the White House unobserved except by a pair of German shepherds, whose handlers curb them swiftly when they bay and lunge at me.

"It is just a cat," one cop says in a tone of disgust, but the dogs know better. Luckily, nobody has much listened to dogs since Lassie was a TV star.

Socks is not officially resident at the Big White until after the swearing in, so I do not expect to find any clue in the vicinity. What I do expect is to be found. When I am, it is a most unexpectedly pleasant experience.

I am near the Justice Building when I hear my name whispered from the shade of a Dumpster. I whirl to see a figure stalking out of the shadow—a slim Havana Brown of impeccable ancestry.

"You the out-of-town muscle?" she asks, eyeing me backwards and forwards with a dismaying amount of doubt.

"My best muscle is not visible," I tell her smugly.

"Oh?" Her supple rear extremity arches into an insulting question mark.

I sit down and stroke my whiskers into place. "In my head."

That stops her. She circles me, pausing to sniff my whiskers, a greeting that need not be intimate but often is. Then she sits in front of me and curls her tail around her sleek little brown toes, paired as tightly as a set of chocolate suede pumps in Miss Temple Barr's closet.

"You know my name," I tell her. "What is yours?"

"You could not pronounce my full, formal name," she informs me with a superior sniff. "My human companions call me Cheetah Habanera for short."

Cheetah, huh? She does look fast, but a bit effete for the undercover game.

"You sure you are not a Havana Red?" I growl.

She shrugs prettily. "Please. My people fled Cuba more than thirty years ago with my grandmother twelve-times removed. I am a citizen, and more than that, my family has been in government work ever since. What have you done to serve your country lately?"

Disdain definitely glimmers in those round orbs the color of old gold.

"They also serve who stand and wait," I quip. An apt quote often stands a fellow in good stead with the opposite sex. Not now.

She eyes my midsection. "More like sit and eat. But you managed to get here quickly, and that is something. Do you know the background of the subject?"

"What has grammar got to do with it?"

"The subject," she says with a bigger sigh, "Socks, is a domestic shorthair, about two years old; nine to ten pounds, slender and supple build." She eyes me again with less than enchantment. "He has yellow eyes; wears black with a white shirtfront, a black face-mask, and, of course, white socks."

"Yeah, yeah. I know the type. A Uni-Que."

"Uni-Que? I never heard of that breed."

"It is not one," I inform her brusquely, "just a common type. That is what I call them. Street name is 'magpie.' I know a hundred guys who look like that. If this Socks wants to lose himself in a crowd, he picked the right color scheme for the job. You, on the other hand—"

"Stick to business," she spits, ruffling her neck fur into a flattering, chocolate brown frill.

I refrain from telling her that she looks beautiful when she is angry. The female of my species is a hard sell who requires convincing even when in the grip of raging hormonal imbalance, and I do mean moan. This one is as cold as the Washington Monument.

"Fixed?" I ask.

"Do you mean has he had a politically correct procedure?

Of course," she answers, "is not everybody 'fixed' these days?"

"Not everybody," I say. "What is the dude's routine?"

"He is not a performing cat—"

"I mean where does he hang out, what jerks his harness?"

"Oh. Squirrels."

"Squirrels?"

"He is from Arkansas. They must have simpler sports there."

"Nothing wrong with a good squirrel chase," I say in the absent dude's defense, "though I myself prefer lizards."

Her nose wrinkles derisively. "We D.C. cats have more serious races on our minds than with squirrels and lizards. Do you know how vital to our cause it is that an intelligent, independent, dignified cat with integrity inhabit the White House, rather than a drooling, run-in-all-directions dog, for the first time in years? The four major animal-protection organizations have named 1993 the Year of the Cat, and the year is off to a disastrous start if Socks does not take residence ASAP."

"Huh? What is ASAP, some political interest group?"

Her lush-lashed eyes shudder shut. "Short for 'As Soon As Possible.' Do Las Vegans know nothing?"

"Only odds, and it looks like Washington, D.C., is odder than anything on the Las Vegas Strip, and that is going some. Okay. We got a late-adolescent ex-tom who is a little squirrelly. Any skeletons in the closet?"

"Like what?"

"Insanity in the family?"

For the first time she is silent, and idly paws the concrete, all the better to exhibit a slim foreleg. I cannot tell if she is merely scratching her dainty pads, or thinking.

"Family unknown," she confesses. "Could be a plant by a foreign government. Odd how neatly he became First Cat of

Arkansas. The Clintons had lost their dog Zeke to an auto accident—"

I nod soberly. "It happens, even to cats."

"The First Offspring, Chelsea, saw two orphaned kittens
outside the house where she took piano lessons and begged
for the one with white socks. The President and his wife are
allergic to cats, but okayed Chelsea taking the male."

"Now that is the most encouraging sign of presidential
timber I have seen yet," I could not help noting. "Ask not
what you can sacrifice for your country when your own president and spouse will suffer stuffy noses so their little girl can
take in a homeless dude. Kind of makes your eyes water."

"Mine are bone dry." Cheetah answers with enough ice in
her tone to frost her brown whiskers white.

"What about the female?" I ask next.

"What female?"

"You said 'the male.' There were two orphans. Ergo, the
other must be female."

She blinks, impressed by my faultless logic and investiga-
tive instincts. No doubt. Then she sighs.

"Taken in too, by a friend of the piano teacher who read
about Socks and also had lost a pet dog. A Republican lady."
She sniffs, whether at the political or former pet leanings of
the other kit's adoptive family, I cannot yell.

"Another Uni-Que?" I ask.

"No." Cheetah Habanera is proving oddly reluctant to reveal Socks's family connections. I soon discover why. "Jet
black. All over. Now called 'Midnight.' "

All right! Methinks a small detour to Arkansas on the way
home might become necessary. I am not politically preju-
diced. Republican cats are still superior to Democratic dogs.
Midnight, huh. Nice name. At least Little Miss Midnight is
not missing.

46

"She is also fixed?" I inquire.

"Who knows? Or cares? Listen, Mr. Midnight, better keep your nose to business. Without Socks found by tomorrow, your name will by *Mudd*night Louie. I do not know why Kitty Kong wanted out-of-town help anyway."

"To catch a thief, send a thief. To find a disoriented, disaffected out-of-towner—"

"Right. If you get a lead on Socks, you can find me here."

She sidles back into the Dumpster shadow like she was born there, and I start looking around Washington. My plan is serendipitous, which is to say, nonexistent.

I pace the terrain, sniff the chill winter air and generally observe how this place would strike a fellow from the country's heartland. Like a monumental chip off the big cold white berg on an iceman's truck.

Miles of hard pavement and towering buildings as white and bland as the grave markers in the National Cemetery would not seem welcoming to a junior good ole boy squirrel-chaser from Little Rock.

One other thing is clear. Not many cats hang out in these sterile public corridors. Even a down-home Uni-Que would stick out like a sore throat.

Naturally, I do not expect to stumble over the absent Socks on my first tour of the place, so I amble over to the Arkansas Ball hotel for some forced-air heat and human company.

The place is a mess of activity, a snarl of hotel minions and party organizers in both senses of the word, a veritable snake pit of electrical cables and audiovisual equipment. Even the Secret Service wouldn't notice a stray cat in this mayhem and I make sure I am not noticeable when I want to be.

Earl E. is jamming onstage with the other boys in the band. (How come there are never girls? Even we cats make our night music coed.) He is rehearsing for the big Arkansas Ball tonight, where you can bet Clinton, Inc. will be even if Socks is missing.

Nose E., wearing a Scotch-plaid vest to protect him from the winter chill, is lying like a discarded powder puff near the Earl E.'s open burgundy-velvet-lined instrument case, eyes the usual; coal black glint behind the haystack hairdo, and black nose pillowed on furry toes. I presume the thing has toes.

I have been out pounding pavement all morning while this fluffpuff has been supine posing for a Johnnie Walker Red ad.

Nose E. gives an obligatory growl of greeting, then admits that he has nothing to do. It seems that Earl E. and his buddies are too busy jiving and massaging their glittering brass saxes onstage to pay Nose E. any mind. Or is that saxi?

That is the trouble with a prima donna dog, whatever the gender: they get addicted to being the center of attention. So would I if I were carried everywhere, wore bows on my ears and was called "Sweetie Pie" by celebrities who never would dream that I am really a cross between a bodyguard and a snitch. Me, I like being Mr. Anonymous and underestimated.

Nose E.'s litany of ills goes on. Nothing is doing until six o'clock or so, he says. He has met his handler of the evening, and it is not the usual scintillating doll in rhinestones, but a former football player who holds him like a dumbbell, with one hammy hand around his rib cage.

Besides, Nose E. notes morosely, so many federal security types decorate the building, and indeed the entire town— they even seal the manholes along the Inauguration parade route—that not even a speck of fairy dust could escape notice. Nose E., in short, is redundant. For such, a spoiled squirt, that is indeed hard to take.

So sunk is Nose E. in his imagined troubles that he does

not think to ask about my mission; besides, to a dude after co-caine and TNT, normal, ordinary canine pursuits, such as finding and harassing cats, is low priority.

This is fine, for my observations during my meander, in which I have seen Socks's puss peeking out from every news-paper-dispensing machine, has given me an idea—not that anybody outside the Clinton inner circle knows that Socks is missing.

What is obvious, if not the whereabouts of Socks, is that this dude's overnight fame has made him a hard slice of sa-lami to hide, no matter how commonplace his appearance. Now I know where to look.

I wander toward the river. I am not much for rivers, but I avoid the public portions bordered by leafless trees and bare expanses of brown green lawn, heading for the fringes where I know I can find a population that inhabits every city—the homeless.

Even the homeless are hard to find in D.C. right now. Pan-handlers know better than to haunt the populated areas when a major network event is unfolding; besides, half of them are dressing and duding up like the rest of the inauguration in-flux, to play Cinderella and Prince Charming-for-a-day at the Homeless Ball.

At last I find a motley group wearing their designer hand-me-downs from Salvatore Arme. In their battered trench coats and tattered sweaters and mufflers, they resemble a huddle of war correspondents.

I do not expect any revelations as to the whereabouts of the missing Socks from these folks, but where the homeless gather, so do their animal companions of choice: dogs. And no one on the city streets knows the scuttlebutt like a dog that associates with a transient person.

Sure enough, I spot a Hispanic man in a cap with numerous news clips safety-pinned to it, surrounded by a bark of dogs, doing same. I look for the unseated Millie of White House fame among them, but these dogs' only visible pedigree is by purée. They are as awkward a conjunction of mutts as I have ever seen and are barking and milling and twining their leashes until they resemble one of those seven-headed monsters of antiquity, but they are at least talkative and really rev up when I stroll into view.

I sit down, making clear that I will not depart without information. The people present view me with alarm, but I am used to being considered unlucky and even dog bait. Besides, should the pack lose their leashes, I have already spied the tree I would climb like a berserk staple gun.

"Cat," these morons yap at me and each other, growing evermore excited. (I do not speak street dog, a debased and monosyllabic language, but I understand enough to get by.)

"Yeah," I growl back, "I suppose you are not used to seeing such fine specimens of felinity."

They claw turf as their whines go up a register. The poor dude in the cap now has his arms twisted straitjacket-style as he tries to control his entourage, all the while yelling, "Scat!"—he pronounces it "Escat!"

The other homeless watch in hopes of some action entertainment shortly.

"Black cat," the dogs carol in chorus after rubbing their joint brain cell together.

"Bingo." I yawn. "See any black and white cats lately?"

They go berserk, baying out cats of all colors that they have seen and pursued. Not one is a magpie.

After a few more seconds of abuse, I am convinced that the street dogs have not sniffed hide nor hair of Socks, luckily for him. Further, I also learn that the humans present are not as ignorant of Socks's newfound celebrity as I had hoped.

A woman with a face as cracked as last year's mud edges toward me, a bare hand stretched out in the chill. "Here, Kitty. Stay away from those dogs. Come on. If you walked through whitewash you'd even look like that there Socks. Here, Kitty," she croons in that seductive tone of entrapment used upon my ancestors for millennia, "I got some food."

I remain amazed that people who have nothing, not even the basic fur coat my kind take for granted, are so eager to take kindred wanderers under their wings.

These homeless individuals may be sad, or deficient in some social or mental way, but they share a certain shrewd survival instinct and camaraderie also found among the legion of homeless of the feline and canine kind. Of course we all need and want a home, but most are not destined for such bounty and are not above appealing to the guilt of the more fortunate in making our lot more palatable. At least the homeless of the human kind are not corralled into the experimental laboratories or the animal-processing pounds that ultimately offer little more than the lethal injection or the gas chamber in the name of mercy.

So I look upon this sweet old doll with fond regret, but I am a free spirit on a mission, and too well-fed (if not well-bred) to take advantage of a kind face despite the temptation of a free meal. I scamper away, leaving the battlefield to the dogs, and trudge back downtown, much dispirited.

If even the homeless have seen enough discarded newspapers to know about Socks, it will prove harder than I thought to turn up the little runaway. Will Socks vanish into the legions of homeless felines from which he came? Will the country and the Clintons survive such a tragic turn of events? Will Midnight Louie strike out?

I picture Cheetah Habanera's piquant but triumphant face as I trot back to Hoopla Central. The sun is shining; the brisk air hovers pleasantly above freezing. For some reason mobs of people are thronging down Pennsylvania Avenue. I manage to thread my way through a berserk bunch performing calisthenics with lawn chairs. People do the strangest things.

Still distracted, I return to the hotel that will host the Clintons' triumphant Arkansas Ball. Everybody in this town has something to celebrate, except for Socks and me.

The stage area is temporarily deserted; even Nose E. is gone, and I shudder to find that I miss the little snitch's foolish face. Earl E.'s instrument case is still cracked open like a fresh clam. I curl up on the burgundy velvet lining—an excellent background for one of my midnight-black leanings—and lose myself in a catnap. Maybe something will come to me in a dream.

The next thing I know, I am being shaken out of my cushy bed like a cockroach out of a shoe.

Earl E. Byrd is leaning over me, his longish locks pomaded into Michael Jackson tendrils and his best diamond earring glittering in one ear. I take in the white shirtfront and the jazzy black leather bolo tie with the real live dead scorpion embedded in acrylic in the slide. Earl E. looks snazzy, but a little shook up.

"The case is for the instrument, dude," he thunders, brushing a few handsome black hairs from the soft velvet. "Behave yourself or you will be ejected from the ball. How did you get here, anyway?"

Of course I am not talking, and I can see by the way the lights, camera, action and musicians are revving up that Earl E. has no time to escort me elsewhere. He has other things on his mind as he lays his precious sax back in my bed. Does a sax feel? Does a sax need shut-eye? Is a sax on a mission to save the First Feline? Is there no justice?

Nose E. comes up to sniff at me in sneering rectitude, and I know that the last question was exceedingly foolish. Before Nose E. can really rub it in, a humongous man in a structurally challenged tuxedo swoops up the little dust bunny and moves into a room that has now filled with women in glitz and glitter and men in my classy colors—black with a touch of white about the face.

Let the ball begin.

Earl E. and the boys swing out. Although Earl E. is essaying the licorice stick at the moment, several musicians bear saxophones that shine brassy gold in the spotlights and wail, I'll admit, like the Forlorn Feline Choir in the darkest, bluesiest, funkiest alley on the planet. Folks foxtrot. The hip . . . hop. I settle grumpily next to the sax case from which I was so rudely evicted. All is lost. On the morrow the nation will wake to the news that it has a new president and a former First Feline. Bast knows—Bast is the Egyptian cat deity and my purrsonal favorite—what Kitty Kong will do.

While I am drowsing morosely, I start when the case beside me jolts. A burp of excitement bubbles just offstage. Someone knocks into Earl E.'s sax. So what. A pair of anonymous hands rights the big, shiny loudmouth thing. I see enough black wingtips to shoe a centipede cluster onto the stage from the wings. When the phalanx of footwear suddenly parts, the First Couple stands there like a King and Queen in a Disney animated feature—Bill and Hillary dancing.

No doubt this is a festive and triumphal scene, and the First Lady's hair is rolled into a snazzy Ginger Rogers do, and they got rhythm and all's right with the world and I could go out in the garden and eat worms . . .

As my bleary eyes balefully regard the hated sax that has usurped my spot, I spy an odd thing. Inside the deep, dark mouth of the instrument something shines—not bright and gold—but whitish silver.

A snake of suspicion stirs in my entrails until it stings my brain fully awake. Why is Earl E. not playing the sax, when he brought it especially for that purpose?

Even as I speculate, Earl E. slips offstage and heads toward me. I expect another ejection, but he ignores me and reaches for the sax, his eyes on the stage where the First Couple has stopped dancing. The President is edging over to the band and microphone. He's going to talk, that is what presidents do, only when they do it, it is an address. He's going to address the crowd . . . my big green eyes flash to the approaching Earl E. The President is going to talk, then Earl E. is going to give him the sax and the President is going to *play* it!

The President is going to play a doctored sax in front of millions of TV-watching citizens.

Even as Earl E. grabs the sax I leap up, all sixteen claws full out and sink them into his arm.

He jumps back and mouths an expression that luckily is frowned out by all the bebopping going on, but it rhymes with "rich" if that word had a male offspring.

I can tell I drew blood, because Earl E. drops his precious sax and it hits the case sideways and something falls out of the mouth like a stale wad of gum.

Earl E.'s eyes get wide and worried. He whirls back to the stage, runs over to appropriate a sax from a startled fellow player and hands it to the President with a flourish.

Everybody plays. Saxophones wail in concert. Everybody laughs and applauds. Something rustles behind me. The Meat locker has returned Nose E. to the vicinity. The creature stiffens on its tiny fuzzy legs as its nose gives several wild twitches. Nose E. rushes toward the fallen sax, sits up and cocks an adorable paw as he tilts his inquisitive little noggin one way, then the other.

Earl E. is over in a flash. This nauseating behavior is Nose E.'s signal that he has smelled a rat. Being an undercover canine, he can resort to nothing obvious like barking. (Besides, he squeaks like a castrated seal.)

Then Earl E. upends the sax to shake out a windfall of plastic baggies containing a substance that much resembles desiccated catnip. I come closer for a look-see, but am rudely shoved aside.

"Good dog," Earl E. croons several sickening times.

What about my early warning system? Except for rubbing a hand on his forearm, he seems to have forgotten my pivotal role in exposing the perfidy. Probably puts it down to mysterious feline behavior.

Two of the wingtips come to crouch beside Earl E., taking custody of the bags, the sax and the case. There goes beddybye.

"Marijuana. Whoever did this," one comments softly, "wanted to make sure that this time the President would inhale."

"Saxophones don't work that way."

"Does not matter," the other wingtip says. "The idea was to embarrass the President. The dog yours?"

"Yeah," Earl E. says modestly.

"Sharp pup." The wingtip pats Nose E. on the cherry red bow.

Sure, the dogs always get the credit.

So I sit there, overlooked and ignored and Sockless, as the party goes on. The President surrenders the sax and the stage and leaves for another inaugural ball. I cannot even get excited at this one when Carole King comes on to sing "You've Got a Friend." Name one.

The band plays on. I recognize a couple tunes, like the ever tasteful "Your Mama Don't Dance and Your Daddy Don't Rock and Roll," and the ever inspirational "Amazing Grace."

I'll say inspirational. I rise amid the postinaugural hubbub and make my silent retreat. Nobody notices.

Outside it is dark, but I have already reconnoitered the city and I know where I am going. There is only one place in town where a dude as overpublicized as Socks Clinton could hang out and be overlooked.

"I once was blind but now I see." I see like a cat in the dark, and I see my unimpeded way to a certain street on which stands a certain civic building. Around back is the obligatory Dumpster.

I wait.

Soon a curious pair of electric green eyes catches a stray beam of sodium iodide streetlight. The dude's white shirt-front and feet look pretty silly tinted mercurochrome pink as he steps out into the sliver of light. He looks okay, for a Uni-Que.

"Why did you do it?" I ask.

"How did you find me?" he retorts instead of answering. Then I realize that the poor dude *has* answered me.

"I figured out that there was only one place you could hang out and beg tidbits without being recognized: The Society for the Blind. Midnight Louie always gets his dude. You have to go back."

"Where? Home? I live in Little Rock."

"Not any more. You are a citizen of the nation now."

"I didn't ask to be First Cat."

I search through my memory bank of cliches but only find "Life is no bed of Rose's." (I do not know who this Rose individual was, but apparently she knew how to take a snooze, and that I can endorse.) I decide to appeal to his emotions.

"It seems to me that your human companion, Miss Chelsea Clinton, faces the same dislocation," I point out. "I would hate to see my delightful roommate, Miss Temple Barr, face a barrage of public curiosity and a new and demanding role in life without my stalwart presence at her side."

"You would move here?" Socks asks incredulously. "Where are you from?"

"Las Vegas."

"Oh," he nods, as if that explains a lot. "I bet you do not even chase squirrels. Did you know the White House squirrels may be . . . rabid?" he adds morosely.

"No!" I respond in horror. There is nothing worse than tainted grub. Poor little guy . . . no wonder he split.

"And," Socks adds in the same spiritless monotone, "you have not had the press shooting pictures down your tonsils for weeks, or getting you high on nip so you'll spill your guts to the press and embarrass your family. Then they dug up some rumor that my father was a notorious tomcat—"

"Shocking! But so was my old man."

"You are not First Feline," he spat glumly. "There's that instant book about me by that name, and all those T-shirts, then menu items named after me in places where I would not even be allowed to lap water. Can you believe that a local hotel concocted a Knock Your Socks Off drink?"

"Sounds like incitement to riot to me. What is in it?"

"Frangelico, Grand Marnier, half-and-half and creme de cacao."

"Does not sound half bad."

"I do not even know what most of those ingredients are. Now if they had made it from Dairy Queen ice cream—"

"Forget Dairy Queens. You are on a faster track now."

"I guess. They dug up some love letters I scratched in the sand to a certain lady named Fleur before I was fixed; I'm only an adolescent, for Morris's sake—I should be allowed some privacy."

"Sacrifice of privacy is a small price to pay considering what you can do for the country and your kind. We need a good role model in a prominent position. You owe your little doll and cats everywhere to stick in there for four years."

"Eight," Socks says, a combative gleam dawning in his yellow eyes.

I swallow a smile (my kind are not supposed to smile or laugh, and I like to keep up appearances) and trot out my more grandiose sentiments. I begin to see that what this dude needs is a campaign speech.

"Remember, Socks, you represent millions of homeless cats, crowded masses yearning to breathe free of the pounds and the lethal streets. We are a transient kind in a world that little notes nor long remembers our welfare. You may not have chosen prominence, but now you can use it to do good. Some are born great," I add, preening, "others have greatness thrust upon them by circumstance. You are one of these . . . circumstantial dudes. Do you want to drive your little doll into such loneliness at your defection that the First Kid goes turncoat and gets a dog to replace you? Do you want to be known as the first First Feline in history to abdicate?"

"No-o-o."

I have him. I brush near, give him a big brotherly tap of the tail on his shoulder. "What is really troubling you, kid? What made you snap and take off just as you got into town?"

Socks sighed. "I have been offered a book contract."

"Hey! That is good. I dabble in that pursuit myself."

"The book is to be called *Socks: The Untold Story*."

I am nudging him down the alleyway and into the full glare

of the street light. The bustle of inaugural traffic rumbles in the distance along with faint sounds of revelry. D.C. could be the Big Easy tonight.

"What is so bad about that?" I ask.

Sock stops. "There is nothing untold left to tell! The press has squeezed every bit of juice out of my own life. I have nothing to say."

"Is that all? Big-time celebrity authors do not let that stop them from penning shoo-in bestsellers. You just think you are not interesting. What you need, my lad, is what they call a 'ghost writer'—someone discreet and more experienced who can help you bring out the most interesting facets of your life."

"Squirrels?"

"No. We must create a feline 'Roots.' We can call it 'Claws.' What do you know about your mom and dad? All cats in this country are descended from the Great Mayflower Mama, of course, but I have heard on good authority that your forebears were mousers around Mount Vernon. Did not Martha Washington herself have a cat-door installed there for somebody's ancestors? Why not yours? Obviously, there is a long tradition of presidential association in your family . . . speaking of which, how about your sister, Midnight—nice name—where in Little Rock did you say she hung out?"

By now I have the dude heavily investing in his new career as raconteur and idol of his race. We reach the White House in no time, and I push him in. He admits that he could use the litter box in the engineering room. Aside from a few distraught aides—and aides are used to being distraught—no one need know of Socks's little escapade.

I trot back to my hotel, anticipating informing that snippy Cheetah Habanera of my success, and contemplating the fifty-fifty book deal I have just cut with Socks. Somebody has got to look out for a naive young dude in this cruel world.

Even though it is late, I have to wait outside the motel room door for at least an hour before Earl E. and Nose E. arrive, both a bit tipsy: Earl E. high on jamming and celebrity, Nose E. on all that marijuana he sniffed out.

I am in like Flynn and ensconced on the king-size before either of them gets a chance at it. Earl E. phones home before he retires, with news of his big adventure, which is how I learn who planted the weed in the presidential saxophone.

"PUFF," Earl E. explains to a benighted buddy on the phone while Nose E., half zonked, tries to curl up near me. I cuff the little spotlight-stealer away. "They called to claim responsibility. Can you believe it, man? PUFF is a radical wing of the pro-smoking types. I do not know what it stands for—People United For Fumes? Whatever, they were ticked off when Clinton made such a big deal about not inhaling once long ago and far away! They think it is un-American and namby-pamby to smoke anything without inhaling. Weird. We have had a weird time in this burg, man. What a gig. I cannot wait to get back to someplace normal like Las Vegas."

Amen.

Letting the Cat out of the Bag

Wendi Lee

Agnes must not be home, Bridie O'Rourke thought as she let herself into the house with a key. Agnes was always there on Thursdays when Bridie came to clean the house. The elderly lady liked her company, and always made cookies and tea for Bridie after she'd done the dishes, vacuumed, and dusted the tiny house.

Odd, thought Bridie as she put her bag of cleaning supplies down, Agnes' cat, Percy, was usually there, twining herself around Bridie's ankles. She glanced in the living room and noted that the television set was gone. She checked the kitchen, calling out as she went down the hall. "Agnes? Are you home?"

She thought she heard something, but it was so faint that she couldn't place it. It took another ten minutes for Bridie to discover Agnes bound and gagged in a closet up in her bedroom. By then, Bridie had realized that her instincts had been right—something was wrong. Numerous antiques, jewelry, paintings and entertainment equipment were missing. She called 911.

It was another fifteen minutes before the paramedics arrived, sirens blaring.

Detective Sid Quinn shuffled some papers, but still couldn't find a pen to sign his arrest report. He sighed. His

61

new partner had "borrowed" his pen again.

Sid rolled his eyes, got up, and went to the supply closet to sign out another box of pens. The lieutenant was right behind him when he turned around. Lieutenant Washington eyed the box of pens in Sid's hand and frowned. "Say, Sid, you operating a black market on pens or something?"

"Nah, they just keep walking off on me," Sid replied.

"Well, remember that the budget review is coming up soon. Put 'em on a leash."

Ha ha, Sid thought. He smiled at Washington and started to return to his desk.

But Washington wasn't done with him yet. "Oh, Sid, by the way, we just got a call in about a burglary up in Fourth and Cedar. You and Pete can handle it."

Sid nodded, went to the dispatcher to get the particulars, and then he and his partner were off.

The scene of the crime was a nice middle-class house made of stucco that looked sort of like those Tudor houses he and his wife Shirley would have seen if she had lived to go to England this summer.

The woman who answered the door was a stout woman with a pleasant face. She identified herself as Bridie O'Rourke, a housekeeper who had worked for Agnes Hughes for two years.

"I've made up a list of what's missing, as far as I can tell," she told Sid, handing him a neatly written sheet of paper.

"Tell me what happened." He handed the list to Pete and took out his notebook. Pete was supervising the fingerprint crew.

Ms. O'Rourke put her hands together and began. "Agnes didn't answer the door today, which was wrong. She always does. She looks forward to my visits as much for the company as for the cleaning."

He nodded, thinking that Bridie O'Rourke looked very capable. He wondered if she had a record. On the outside, she looked like a nice enough person, but he'd learned long ago that looks were deceiving.

"I first noticed that the television was gone, of course, because it's in the living room and that's the first room I see when I come in the front door." She walked toward the front and indicated the room. It was neat and didn't look as if it needed cleaning. There was a bare surface on a small oak entertainment center.

"We'll dust for fingerprints," he assured her.

She nodded. "Well, I thought she might have had it taken in to be repaired. She'd been complaining about the picture lately, so I didn't think anything of it." The housekeeper walked back to the kitchen. "It was in here that I first heard a noise. It sounded human. I looked around for Percy—"

"Percy?"

"Her cat. Percy likes to sleep in odd places—empty shopping bags, piles of clean laundry, the dryer—"

"The dryer?" Sid asked.

Bridie O'Rourke nodded. "She's been known to sleep in small, enclosed spaces. Sometimes we've searched for hours, looking for her. Agnes gets worried if she doesn't see Percy for some time. That cat has actually been carried away in someone's handbag before. Scared the poor woman half to death when she opened the bag and found a cat curled up in her purse."

Sid felt the housekeeper was wandering off the subject, so he cut the interview short by clapping his notebook shut. "Well, thank you for your time, Ms. O'Rourke. We'll contact you with further questions." After all, she hadn't actually seen the burglars.

Two high spots appeared on her cheeks. She'd seemed

about to say something, probably about his being rude, but she gave him a tight smile instead, turned on her heel and left.

The nerve of that man, Bridie thought as she gathered her cleaning supplies to leave. He'd cut her off, just as she was getting to the good part of the story. And it might have helped him with his case. She took a deep breath when she got out of the house and headed for her car. She might as well go to the hospital to see how Agnes was doing. Maybe she'd get there ahead of that rude detective.

Twenty minutes later, Bridie crept into Agnes Hughes's room. Her employer wore a hospital robe with little blue flowers all over it. She had a bruise over her right cheekbone, but otherwise looked to be in good spirits, if a little frail.

Bridie always thought Agnes could have auditioned for the part of Miss Marple. She was in her sixties, had fluffy white hair and rouged cheeks. Her blue eyes twinkled on a good day, but this hadn't been such a day. Instead, she was wringing her soft blue-veined hands.

"You're finally here. They've poked and prodded me and pronounced me sound, but old," Agnes Hughes said. "And they won't let me leave. The nurse told me that the doctor wants to observe me overnight."

Bridie smiled and reached out to gently squeeze one of her friend's hands. "I'm just so glad you're all right, Agnes."

The elder woman shrugged. "I'm a tough old bird." Her eyes were anxious. "Bridie, is Percy all right?"

Bridie frowned. This was going to be the hard part, telling Agnes she'd searched all over the house for Percy, but the cat couldn't be found.

Detective Sid Quinn found Agnes Hughes's hospital room and knocked with purpose before stepping inside. He found the housekeeper sitting on the bed, comforting the elderly woman.

"What am I going to do without Percy?" the old woman cried.

"We'll find your cat for you. She probably just ran off when the burglar was taking things out of your house." Both women looked up as the detective approached the bed. He glared at Bridie O'Rourke. "I'm sorry, ma'am, but I'm here on official business, and I'm going to have to ask you to leave."

"Oh, please, Detective," Agnes Hughes said, "she's my friend and I don't think I can stand to be alone right now."

Just his luck—the housekeeper had this woman in the palm of her hand. On a hunch, Sid had his partner Pete check Bridie O'Rourke back at the precinct and he'd come up with a long rap sheet. The woman was a veritable crime spree when it came to larceny, bad checks, and conning the elderly. She had grown up in Driscoll, a small community outside of Raleigh where everyone was related to everyone else, and they were all thieves and con men.

"Um, I'm going to ask Ms. O'Rourke to leave the room to, um, get us some coffee." He turned to the housekeeper and gave her his best grin. "You wouldn't mind, would you?"

Her eyes turned steely. He would swear she knew what he was thinking. But she stood up, her dignity intact, and asked, "Do you take it black or with cream and sugar?"

Bridie was seething when she left the room. It was clear he'd found out about her past, but instead of confronting her, he'd ordered her to get coffee, as if she were a maid. Agnes knew about her past, so it wouldn't come as a shock when Detective Quinn offered Bridie up as a suspect.

She went to the hospital cafeteria to order the coffee.

Although Bridie knew that Agnes knew of her past, Bridie wasn't sure how Agnes would react—would she brush the detective's accusations aside or would she have second thoughts about her housekeeper? The truth of the matter was that Bridie wasn't sure what to think about her own past.

The detective and Agnes looked up when she knocked and entered with the three coffees. Agnes winked at her, and Bridie felt a burden lifted—at least one person still believed in her.

Detective Quinn, on the other hand, gave her a stern look. "I was just about to ask Mrs. Hughes some questions. Could you leave the coffees and go out to the waiting area?"

"But Detective, there's something you should know about Percy—" Bridie started to say.

Detective Quinn put a hand up. "I'm sure the cat will find its way home. In the meantime, please wait outside."

Bridie bit her lip, choking back a rude retort, and left the room.

Sid watched the housekeeper leave. Then he turned back to Agnes Hughes. "Now, Mrs. Hughes, can you tell us anything about the intruder, anything at all?"

Mrs. Hughes's lips were set in a thin line. He'd already had an earful about the housekeeper and what a friend she was to the old woman. Agnes Hughes had started to tell him about her cat, Percy, but since he wasn't in the cat-finding business, he'd cut her off as well. He was there to find the intruder and arrest him or her.

"Detective, can I tell you one thing, please?"

He sighed, wanting to get the description of the intruder and get to work on the case. "All right, Mrs. Hughes, but keep it short. We need a description of the person who assaulted you so we can put an APB through dispatch."

"My cat, she likes to sleep in small, dark places. Well, one time, I spent hours trying to find her. I finally came across her asleep in the overnight case I'd just unpacked. Anyway, what I wanted to tell you—"

Sid surreptitiously looked at his watch, then smiled and interrupted her. "Mrs. Hughes," he said gently, "just tell me who has stopped by your place over the last day or two."

Bridie couldn't help the fact that she had good hearing. The doors to the hospital rooms were made of cardboard as far as she was concerned. So she heard how the detective treated her employer, as if she were a doddering old woman. Bridie crossed her arms, intent on giving Detective Quinn a piece of her mind when he came out of that room.

She stored the overheard information Agnes Hughes gave Detective Quinn in the back of her mind, a list of people who had stopped by. Two of them, an older man and a man about Bridie's age, sounded very familiar to her. She had an idea who had broken into her employer's place.

When Detective Quinn came out of the room, it startled her. He looked amused that he'd made her jump. "You hear anything good?"

"I didn't like the part where you brushed off the story about the cat. You should have heard her out."

He raised his eyebrows. "That the cat likes to hide in small dark places? I get the picture. The burglar probably has the cat in his bag. It'll make him or her that much easier to find. Good day, Ms. O'Rourke." With that, he brushed past her and headed toward the entrance.

Bridie was fuming. She'd tried to tell him, and so had Agnes Hughes. And now, she'd just tried again and he wasn't listening. Bridie stamped her foot and decided she had to take matters into her own hands. Agnes' description of the two men who had tried to sell her on getting her driveway paved had hit home. She had wanted to take the information to Detective Quinn, but the way he'd listened to her the last few times she'd tried to tell him something important, she'd be better off doing it herself. Besides, he wouldn't get very far on his own. He needed her on the inside. But she knew if she took the information to him, he'd be too suspicious to let her do things her way.

She visited with Agnes Hughes briefly, but her mind was elsewhere, trying to concoct a way back into her past, the past she'd put behind her.

Before Bridie left, she outlined her plan to Agnes.

"Bridie, it's too dangerous," Agnes' voice quavered with fear. "Let the police handle it. I don't want you going back to that awful place."

Bridie let out a frustrated sigh. "If I don't, it'll never get done and Percy is in danger. We need to get her back for you. I won't try any heroics. I just want to get Percy back. Then we can call the police."

Agnes squeezed her friend's hand. "You're a stubborn woman, Bridie. Be careful. You may not be accepted back into the fold."

Bridie knew it would be dangerous, but she had family there. She'd grown up in Driscoll, a town owned by an Irish clan of settled gypsies. They called themselves the Travelers. Driscoll was owned and operated as a closed community, and everyone in that community grew up to become thieves and con artists.

Bridie had grown up among people who thought nothing of bilking elderly men out of their life's savings. It was commonplace to make a living by pretending to be a telemarketer and, with the promise of a nonexistent prize, get a credit card number from a lonely widow or shut-in.

In her late twenties, Bridie was finally caught in one of her schemes and served time in prison for it. When she was released, she was ordered to stay out of her own town, and put on parole. It took time, but she soon realized that her life had been built on lies, deceit, and on other people's misery. Bridie found work as a housekeeper, and had been off parole for the last year.

The next morning, Bridie was ready to go back home, even if it meant going against the court order. She hadn't missed her family much, but she found herself dressing up for the occasion nevertheless—no one in Driscoll could know why she was really there.

Her parents' house was the same, an exercise in excess. Doric columns graced the front of the house, along with frilly Victorian additions and modern windows. The house was a Tudor-style stucco, and painted an awful Pepto Bismol pink. She pulled her five-year-old Celica up the driveway and got out of the car.

Her mother came out first, screaming with delight. "Bridie, you're home! Finally, they let you out of that awful place." Eilish O'Rourke was a tiny woman who had kept her figure and wore the frilliest lace dresses. She looked like a cross between a Southern belle and a frosted wedding cake. Her hair was a large helmet on her small head, as if someone had pumped it up with hair to the point of bursting. Still, it was good to see her mother. She smelled like gardenias in late spring.

Her father was next. He was a gray man, his hair, his eyes, his skin, his teeth. But he had a great sense of humor and she was happy to see him as well.

"Where's the rest of the family?" Bridie asked once they were settled on the veranda with glasses of icy cold lemonade.

"Sean's working right now, and your sister Mary is getting ready for her wedding." Her mother leaned forward and squeezed Bridie's hand. "You came back just in time." A frown marred her expression. "Was it awful in there, Bridie? I wish our lawyer had been able to cut a better deal—"

"Mama, it's fine. I didn't mind doing the time. I met some interesting characters." She searched her mind for some way to introduce the subject without raising suspicion. It didn't take her long to work it into a question. "So, who's working Raleigh these days?"

Her father answered. "That would be the Murphys. You know, Bridie, I'd always hoped you'd marry into the Murphys. They're a good family. Well-to-do, and I think young Johnny's had his eye on you for some time." Most families arranged marriages between family members when they were just children. Bridie had been lucky—her parents had allowed her to skip that ceremony.

Bridie tried hard to smile. She remembered young Johnny, who would have to be in his early thirties by now, and when she last saw him ten years ago, he had two gold incisors and a glass eye from an accident as a child. She wondered which eye he'd had on her—the good one or the glass one.

"When did you get out?" her mother asked.

"About two years ago. I was on parole for a year, and have been ordered to stay away from here. But I couldn't stand it any longer. I had to come see my family. I missed you."

Her father clapped his hands on his knees and stood up. "That does it, then. We'll have a homecoming for you—get everyone together tonight. My daughter's finally home."

"Maybe that Johnny Murphy will ask you to dance," her mother giggled.

The party began at eight o'clock that night. It was amazing

to Bridie how quickly her parents had gotten a party together. Her father had found a Ceilleagh band on short notice, and there were slabs of corned beef and cold poached salmon, mounds of bubble and squeak, Irish soda bread and strawberry tarts, and of course, lots of Guinness. The party was taking place in the back yard, and it was a hot night. Citron candles burned, keeping the mosquitoes and gnats away for the most part.

Someone slapped Bridie on the back. "Good to see you, girl!" Ben Murphy, the head of the Murphy clan, exclaimed. "Johnny'll be along any moment. We had an exciting day."

"Oh?" She knew that polite interest would open the tightest lips. Ben Murphy wasn't even close to the championship title for the tightest lips. He opened up like a cheap ziplock baggie.

"Ah, we started by offering to paint a barn and we made well over seven hundred on that job. Only took us three hours and a little paint." Bridie knew the scam—the cheapest water-based paint, the quickest job, and you got out of there before the customer discovered what a lousy job had been done.

"Oh, good," she murmured.

"After that, we sold a driveway paving to an elderly couple. Cost them a thousand in cash, and they had it stored in a shoebox." Ben shook his head. "In a shoebox, girl! Can you imagine?"

"Bridie!" Johnny Murphy came up to her and gave her a quick hug.

"I'll leave you two young people alone." Ben Murphy sauntered off.

"So tell me, Bridie, you're living in Raleigh now?"

She gave him a quick version of how she came to stay in

Raleigh after she'd been released from prison. "That's terrible," Johnny said.

She noticed he wore long sleeves, even in the heat of a summer night. "Aren't you a bit hot in that?" she asked.

He rubbed his forearm ruefully. "I've gotten a few recent scars from my work. Do you know anyone who wants a cat? I've got one by accident." And he proceeded to tell her all about taking Agnes Hughes for all she was worth.

Bridie tried not to let the revulsion show in her face, but found it difficult. When he finished, she nodded. "I'll take the cat off your hands. I've been wanting a companion."

He gestured for her to follow him. When they got to his van, which was parked in front of the house, he opened the sliding doors. "There's one thing you might want to know about it," he started to say when suddenly police sirens came on and official cars pulled up. Several police got out of their vehicles.

"Put your hands where I can see them," an officer shouted into the bullhorn. Bridie complied, as did Johnny. Bridie could see that Johnny's van was full of Agnes's antiques, her television set, and other things.

Officers swarmed over the van. Bridie tried to warn them. "Officer, there's something you should know—"

One of the officers turned to his partner and said, "Shut her up, will you?"

The other officer turned to Bridie. "Yeah, yeah, we've heard it all. You're just an innocent bystander. You want to talk to your lawyer."

Wouldn't anyone listen? Bridie wondered. Would she spend the next few nights in jail until Agnes got her out, or would they convince her employer that she, Bridie, was bad news?

Another car pulled up, this time with Detective Quinn in

it. Bridie wasn't very happy to see him until Agnes got out of the passenger side.

A yeowl could be heard from the inside of the van.

The officer who'd been leaning inside the van to eye the stolen property now jumped back. "Ow! Get this damn cat off me. What's going on here?" He'd been so rude to Bridie, she couldn't help feeling some satisfaction from watching him dance around with Percy clawing his arm. If he'd listened to her, he wouldn't have tried to wake the cat.

Sid watched the circus in front of Bridie O'Rourke's parents' house. He was relieved when Agnes stepped forward and gently removed the small gray and orange tiger cat from the officer's arm. Then she went over to Bridie, who was being handcuffed and read her rights by another police officer. Sid stepped up and grabbed one of Bridie's arms. "I'll take this one, officer. She's violated a court order to stay away from Driscoll."

The officer tipped his hat to Sid. "Whatever you say, detective."

Sid guided Bridie into his backseat, then helped Agnes in beside her, handing Percy to her. The tiger cat yawned, stretched, then settled into Agnes Hughes' lap. As they drove off, he handed the handcuff keys back to Agnes. "Will you help your friend get those cuffs off? They get mighty uncomfortable after a while."

Bridie's mouth hung open. "You're letting me go?" Agnes had the cuffs off in the twinkle of an eye.

"You were working undercover for us, weren't you?" He glanced in the rear view mirror and thought she was kind of attractive.

"You finally got him to listen," she said to Agnes.

The older woman laughed. "Finally."

"I've never had a seventy-year-old woman tell me to shut my yap before," Sid added. "Kind of made me think twice, and in that amount of time, she was able to tell me enough to get me thinking. You took quite a risk, Ms. O'Rourke."

She shrugged. "They're my people, even if I don't belong there anymore."

"How long do you think they'll be in the pokey, Detective?" Agnes asked.

He laughed again, and Bridie joined her.

"It's been my experience that the Travelers have no trouble getting out of jail because their lawyers are just so damn good."

When Bridie O'Rourke smiled, she was almost pretty, Sid thought.

"Oh, with Agnes' testimony, I don't think the court will have any trouble convicting them," Bridie replied. "Besides, Johnny Murphy has scratches up and down his right arm. That's why he was wearing long sleeves in this heat." Sid made a mental note to have photographs taken of Johnny Murphy's scratches.

"Idiot! You should never wake a sleeping cat," Agnes muttered indignantly.

"Now how does that go again?" Sid asked. "Tell me the full story, Mrs. Hughes. I'm afraid I wasn't listening very closely after you mentioned that Bridie had gone to Driscoll to rescue Percy who, I might add, didn't seem to need much rescuing after all."

Bridie giggled at his humor, and damned if she wasn't downright pretty. Anyone who laughed at his lame jokes should be asked to dinner.

Agnes hesitated, then said, "Well, Percy is kind of special. I picked her out at the Humane Society when I was feeling especially lonely. I was warned that she had some quirks."

Bridie picked up the story from there. "Such as, she likes to sleep in small, dark places like boxes and bags. And her strangest quirk is that she can't be startled awake. It must have been some trauma when she was a kitten."

"What happens?" Sid asked, even though he'd witnessed Percy's rude awakening. He was enjoying himself for the first time in a long time.

"When she's startled, she lashes out." Agnes rubbed her wrist absently. "She clawed me the first time I made that mistake. Now I put on some Brahms or Beethoven and wait for her to wake up by herself."

Sid chuckled. When they reached Mrs. Hughes's house, he escorted both her and Percy into the house, making sure that everything was safe. "I'll be in touch tomorrow about your things, and about pressing charges against the Murphys. I have a feeling they'll be tied up today just trying to explain away the scratches."

He turned to Bridie O'Rourke. "Would you like a ride home, Ms. O'Rourke?"

She hesitated, looking at Agnes, whose eyes were twinkling. "You go on, Bridie. It's been a long day."

"I'll be back tomorrow to really clean your house," Bridie replied. "I suppose, since you've impounded my car, that I'll have to depend on your kindness."

"I'll sign your car out tomorrow and take care of you until then," he assured her.

As they walked back to his car, Sid said, "I feel I owe you dinner, Ms. O'Rourke. I was rude and should have listened to you."

She gave him a rueful look. "I don't think you could have infiltrated Driscoll without my help, Detective. It's a very closed community. And I appreciate the fact that you didn't reveal the fact that I was there to get the cat for Agnes."

Sid understood—they were still her family and she didn't want to cut all ties.

"I agree," he said. "Your help was necessary, and I'll try to keep you from having to testify. After all, they are still family to you. By the way, call me Sid."

She smiled. "Call me Bridie, Sid."

Nothing But the Best

Brian Lawrence

The cat sniffed the overweight math teacher's face and pulled back quickly. He'd smelled that odor on a human once before, and that time his companion, Mrs. Connors, failed to get up the next morning and put out his Fancy Feast. Nor did she get up the next morning, or the next. The smell had worsened, finally forcing the cat to leave the house he'd grown up in.

"What's you got there, Cisco?" Winslow asked.

Cisco trotted over to the old black janitor and rubbed his head along the man's leg, then sat and washed his face with the back of his paw, trying to eliminate that awful stench.

"Cisco" was not his original name, that had been "Shadow," due to his dark gray coat. But ever since Winslow found him rummaging through the high school's garbage, he'd been called: "The Cisco Cat."

Two years ago, Winslow had been watching a western on his old black and white in the school's basement. During a commercial, he went outside to empty a trash bin and discovered the cat. Cisco arched his back, spat, and hissed at the strange, black man, refusing to relinquish the half-eaten peanut butter sandwich he'd found.

Winslow had just smiled at him and said, "Well, who are you, Cisco the Cat?" Then, surprisingly, the janitor reached out and scooped him up, saying, "Why don't you come on in

77

out of the cold and get some real food."

That night had been Cisco's first can of tuna.

The name stuck and Cisco stayed. Though he had grown fond of the name "Shadow," the janitor could call him anything he wanted as long as the cans of tuna kept coming.

"Well, lordy be, Cisco. It's Mr. Lewis, the math teacher." Winslow bent, his knees cracking in the silent basement. "And I believe he's dead."

Cisco stopped washing and regarded the prone math teacher, who doubled as the track coach, which explained the maroon and yellow sweat suit. Having little else to do until Winslow started his rounds, he decided to investigate.

He gave the corpse wide berth and trotted past, then sniffed the cement floor beyond, picking up the trail, which he followed through the basement to the back stairs, up the cracked concrete steps, and into the west hallway on the first floor. Winslow hadn't yet waxed the white tile hall, which allowed Cisco to easily pick out the two shoulder-width, parallel lines left by the math teacher's track shoes. They cut through the day's collection of scuff marks and footprints, and lead straight to the math teacher's classroom. He followed the trail and stopped at the room's closed door, then sat and pondered the situation while licking his back.

A few moments later, after concluding that someone had dragged Mr. Lewis through the hall and dumped him in the basement for poor Winslow to clean up, Cisco returned to check on his friend. The janitor was talking on the telephone, to the police the cat presumed, so he hunkered down behind the boiler where it was nice and toasty and waited.

Cisco learned three things while the police and the medical examiner were there. First, Mr. Lewis had died approximately two to four hours ago. That would mean between 6:00

P.M. and 8:00 P.M. Second, he was killed by a blow to the head with a heavy, sharp object. And finally, the Cherry Grove, Missouri Police Department was not NYPD Blue.

They had no idea why the math teacher had been in the basement, though Police Chief Anderson did comment on the lack of blood and the possibility Mr. Lewis was killed elsewhere. They'd searched the math teacher's classroom, but had found nothing to help explain the crime. They failed to come up with a motive or a suspect, so they left, telling Winslow to keep his eyes and ears open, and that they'd return in the morning to interview the other teachers.

Winslow nodded, then prepared for his rounds.

Around midnight, Winslow weaved through the empty classrooms dusting and straightening. Cisco followed and listened to his friend's litany.

"You know, Cisco, if my Emily was alive, she'd know how to deal with this situation. Imagine that." He shook his head. "Mr. Lewis murdered right here at Benjamin Franklin High School. Ain't no one ever been murdered in Cherry Grove far as I recall, let alone in the high school. I just don't know what to think, Cisco. Just don't know what to think."

Winslow knelt and ran a callused hand over the cat's back. Cisco arched, purred, and rubbed Winslow's leg. Always treat the source of food well. Mrs. Connors had taught him that.

With the dusting and straightening completed, they started on Cisco's favorite activity, emptying wastebaskets. Time for the midnight buffet.

Winslow pushed the large gray trash bin down the hall, the left wheel squeaking, the right one rattling—it was slightly bent—and stopped at Ms. White's classroom. He opened the Freshman English teacher's door and Cisco dashed in. The cat stuck his nose in the wastebasket, but found nothing appealing, so he stepped aside and let Winslow take the trash and empty it in the trash bin.

They repeated the ritual several times with equally disappointing results, finally reaching Mr. Lewis' classroom. Double bonus time, for not only did Mr. Lewis have a wastebasket—which tonight was empty, the police having taken the contents—but there was a tall, lidded trash barrel outside his room—which the police had overlooked—for the kids to discard wrappers, unfinished snacks, and other culinary delights. Rarely did this trash barrel disappoint Cisco, and tonight was no exception.

He caught the whiff of Nacho Cheese Doritos, one of his favorites. Winslow pulled off the top of the barrel and emptied it into the trash bin. Cisco leaped in after and quickly found the half-full bag of chips.

While munching contentedly on a slightly stale Dorito, he glanced around at the other trash to fill the time. A rumpled sheet of paper caught his attention. He couldn't read it—that he'd not learned—but the row of numbers followed by letters looked familiar. He'd seen something like that before when he'd watched the kids from the air-conditioning vents, only the kids had written the letters. On this paper, both the numbers and the letters were typed. His feline intuition rippled down his spine. Maybe Winslow could find some significance in the piece of paper.

He abandoned his chips and grasped the sheet of paper in his mouth, then leaped out of the trash bin and deposited the paper at Winslow's feet.

"Now why'd you go and do that, Cisco?" Winslow bent and picked up the paper. He started to toss it back into the bin, but Cisco reared and dug his front claws into the old man's leg.

"Ouch! What was that for?"

No answer from Cisco. Winslow shook his head and went to toss the paper away, but again, Cisco struck.

"Ouch! Cisco, this ain't like you." He regarded the cat with sad, brown eyes, and ran a hand over his short, graying hair. "Hmm, maybe you're trying to tell me something."

Cisco rubbed his leg.

Winslow examined the paper. He looked at Cisco, back at the paper, and then back at the cat.

"This is odd, Cisco. You know what this is? It's an answer key for one of Mr. Lewis' tests. Now, I didn't know Mr. Lewis that well, but he certainly wouldn't go throwing away a recent answer key. I would think he'd shred it, wouldn't you?"

Again, Cisco rubbed the man's leg.

"I wonder," Winslow said.

He walked into Mr. Lewis' classroom and sat at the dead teacher's desk. Taking out his skeleton key for all the desks and file cabinets, he unlocked the top left drawer, and removed a grade book, which he put on the desk and opened. Cisco jumped onto the desk and watched. For several minutes, Winslow paged through the book, occasionally consulting the answer key.

"Here it is, Cisco. This year's mid-term." He ran his finger down a column of letters. "Well, I'll be. Look at this."

Cisco looked, but had no idea at what.

"Two students got perfect scores on this test. One is Bobby Tinsdale. You know, the principal's son?"

Cisco knew the spoiled brat, and he laughed to himself remembering that Bobby had recently lost his driver's license. He'd heard the other kids teasing Bobby about being a lead-foot. Third speeding ticket. Suspension of license for six months. Served him right.

"I'd expect that. Straight A student, Bobby is. Mr.

Tinsdale's always bragging on his son, always saying how he's going to go to M.I.T., going to become an engineer."

Winslow looked wistfully up at Cisco. The cat sat still as a statue, giving his friend his full attention, ears turned forward, blue eyes steady.

"Did I ever tell you about my son, LeRoy? He's an engineer. A chemical engineer. Works in plants designing processes to mix things. Smart boy. Got it from his mother. Sure hope he and his family are coming for Easter this year. As long as those plane fares stay down. Why I remember—"

Cisco dipped his head and pawed at the grade book. Enough story-telling. He wanted to know the other name. Bobby Tinsdale made a poor suspect. The boy was short and thin as a rail, a long distance runner for the track team. No way he could drag the hefty Mr. Lewis down to the basement.

Winslow got the hint.

"But look at this other name, Cisco. Ben Ramsey. Nasty, mean boy. Such a shame, too. Used to be a star football player. Then just up and quit. But I don't think he's much of a student. So this here perfect score sure seems suspicious to me. What do you think?"

Cisco thought he should investigate a smell that had been bothering him since they'd entered Mr. Lewis' classroom.

Through the lingering odor of Chief Anderson's English Leather, Cisco smelled blood.

He leaped from the desk and circled the room. On the floor, the smell diminished, overwhelmed by the odor of ammonia. Above him, that's where it came from. He sat and scanned the room.

On the bookcase. He leaped. It was on the track trophy. State champions, 1996, the year Cisco arrived. He sniffed the trophy and found the blood on the corner of the marble base, just a small spot, easily overlooked, especially by Cherry

Grove's finest. He stood on his back legs to smell the top part, where the gold runner was, and knocked the trophy over.

"Cisco, now what are you doing?" Winslow came over and picked up the trophy. He examined it closely. "Well, well. This sure looks like blood." Winslow dropped the trophy, a worried expression clouding his face. "And now look what I done, got my fingerprints on it."

Cisco leaped down from the bookcase and sniffed the top of the trophy. Through his friend's scent, he smelled someone else. Not Ben Ramsey. That was a smell he knew well, having run into the boy in the fall.

He'd been trotting through the school one evening, thinking of the cafeteria trash and not expecting anyone else to be around, when he turned a corner and bumped into Ramsey. The boy kicked out. Cisco dodged, swiped the kid's leg, and bolted back toward the basement. Last time he went into the school hallways without Winslow.

But it wasn't the big ex-football player's scent on that trophy. Whose was it? He thought that answer would be found in connection to the answer key. And grades. He trotted to Mr. Lewis' desk and hopped up, then pawed through the pages.

"Now, what's you doing? You sure acting strange tonight." The old man sat in the teacher's chair and examined the book.

"Look at this, Cisco," Winslow said. "There was only one other test so far this semester. Ben Ramsey got only one wrong. Probably cheated again."

As much as he hated the oversized loser, Cisco felt his friend was giving the boy a bum rap.

Winslow continued. "But look at Bobby Tinsdale's score. Only a fifty-two. Hmm, I wonder."

Winslow left Mr. Lewis' room with Cisco trotting close behind.

They went into Ms. Alexander's room. She was the Senior Honors English teacher. Again, Winslow unlocked the desk and pulled out the grade book.

After a few minutes of flipping through the pages, the janitor said, "This just don't make sense. Don't make no sense at all. Ben Ramsey is in this class. Now, who would have thunk that? He's an honors student?" The old man shook his head. "Of course, Bobby Tinsdale's in here, but all his test scores are terrible, yet his mid-term grade is an A. Don't make no sense."

And it didn't make sense to Winslow when they found the same pattern in three other classrooms. Ben Ramsey and Bobby Tinsdale were in all three classes together. Ben had good test scores and all A's. But Bobby also had all A's, yet lousy test scores.

"It just don't make sense, Cisco," Winslow said, slumped in the chair of Mr. Feasler, the chemistry teacher.

But it did to Cisco. Perfect sense. He leaped off the desk and trotted into the hallway.

"Where you going, Cisco?"

The cat headed toward the office, hoping to find the missing link that would put this case away. The heavy foot-falls of the janitor's boots followed. At the office, Cisco pawed at the door until Winslow reached him.

"You want to go in here? Doubt Mr. Tinsdale threw anything away worth eating."

Cisco scratched again. For once, he wasn't thinking about his stomach.

"Well, okay. Might as well clean the office while we're here. But what about Mr. Lewis? Don't you want to figure out who killed the poor man?"

Cisco bolted through the door as soon as Winslow cracked it open. The smell of blood was overpowering, at least to his nose. He doubted Winslow noticed anything. The cat knew immediately where the smell came from. When he reached the wastebasket by the principal's desk, he hooked a paw over the rim and spilled the contents onto the floor.

"Cisco! I swear, it must be a full moon tonight." Winslow started picking up the trash.

Cisco pushed aside wadded forms, discarded note paper, and a crumpled brown paper bag. The bag had been particularly hard to ignore as his feline nose detected the remains of a tuna sandwich.

All the way at the bottom of the wastebasket he found the source of the smell. He grabbed a large ball of paper-towels and backed out of the wastebasket, again eyeing the brown paper bag. Maybe later.

When he was clear of the debris, he pawed at the bundle, trying to unwrap the ball of paper.

"What's you got?"

Cisco backed away from the wad, and Winslow grabbed it, and started unwrapping it.

"Oh, my." He dropped the wad of paper as if it had bit him.

In the center of the large ball were several paper-towels soaked with blood. Mr. Lewis' blood, Cisco knew. He also knew the smell on the trophy. It matched the smell in the principal's office. Mr. Tinsdale.

When Mr. Tinsdale returned from lunch, a nasty surprise waited for him. Police Chief Anderson and two officers greeted Tinsdale with a warrant for his arrest, charging him with the murder of Mr. Lewis, the evidence having been provided by Winslow. Well, really by Cisco, but the cat didn't mind his friend getting the credit, as long as he got the tuna.

Cisco sat in the air-conditioning vent and watched the arrest. Near as he could figure, Mr. Tinsdale had hung around the school last night waiting for Bobby to finish track practice. With no license, the boy needed a ride home. Mr. Lewis must have seen Tinsdale and had taken the opportunity to confront his boss with Bobby's school performance. Apparently, Mr. Lewis was the one teacher who would not go along with Mr. Tinsdale's scheme.

The police had questioned the other teachers and had discovered that Tinsdale based their raises and their employment status on their willingness to ensure Bobby got all A's. Last night, Mr. Lewis must have said something to indicate he would blow the whistle on Tinsdale, and the principal had panicked, then clobbered the math teacher with the track trophy. Tinsdale was a big man, so he had no trouble dragging Mr. Lewis to the basement.

The principal must have figured there was little chance of being caught, as the school would have been empty, and Winslow didn't come on until 10:00. Only Tinsdale hadn't counted on Cisco's nose.

Chief Anderson snapped the cuffs onto Mr. Tinsdale and led him out of the office.

Cisco heard the principal wail, "I only wanted the best for my son. Only the best. I was just being a good father. My boy deserves nothing but the best."

Cisco returned to the basement, knowing the best waited for him. A warm spot behind the furnace and a fresh can of tuna.

Tall Man, Large Cat

Mat Coward

Easily the dullest work I've ever done in my life is bodyguarding. I did a lot of it a few years back and, apart from that one time when it got a bit exciting, all it consisted of was sitting around in hotel corridors, trying not to fall asleep. Money was good, mind.

I was nineteen years old, studying at a London catering college. I got a government grant, which in a short month just about covered my rent, but for the true essentials—beer, smokes, music—I had to pay my own way. I was always open to suggestions.

"You're tall," Janet from the employment agency said, in answer to my question—which had been, "What qualifications do I have to be a bodyguard?"

"And you're in decent enough shape, aren't you? I know you go swimming a lot."

I did. It was a great way to meet girls. Apparently it had an unpredicted side effect—keeping me fit. As a dedicated slacker I wasn't sure how I felt about that.

I wasn't sure how I felt about being a bodyguard, either. "Janet, you've got me some good jobs in the past. But bodyguarding? That sounds a little serious for my tastes."

She shook her head. "Alan, sweetie, would I put you up for anything dangerous? You're one of my best boys. Trust me, bodyguarding film stars has nothing to do with guarding bodies."

"Ah," I said. "Hence the name."

"It's just another status thing, lovey. These Hollywood types, they have to have their penthouse suites and their personal aromatherapists and their tall young men with sunglasses on. No one's going to try and shoot you. Promise. You're just there for the look of the thing. If they wanted real protection, they'd bring their own people over from the States."

I still wasn't convinced—until Jenny told me the hourly rate, and I suddenly realised that it was my patriotic duty to serve these visiting cinematic artistes to the best of my ability.

No doubt the Americans thought they were gouging the simple natives, but then they probably didn't realise that the highly-experienced, professional bodyguards they were getting were actually moonlighting students who happened to be taller than average. The world, I've noticed, is full of people who think they're ripping each other off—when in actual fact, they're being ripped off by each other.

Pixie O'Quark and Dom Frost were in the UK to promote the first picture they'd made together since they'd got married (to each other, I mean) on a beach in Hawaii. The film was about two gorgeous movie stars who get married on a beach in Barbados. Hollywood, huh—how do they keep coming up with these fresh ideas? The stars and their retinue were booked into the entire fourth floor of Arthurton's Hotel in the West End.

I was allocated midnight to eight in the morning, which would allow me to go straight on to college after my shift ended, and then get a couple of hours sleep in the early evening. The man I was relieving was a small, tough-looking

Arabic guy, who introduced himself as George. He was studying economics at London University. He was envious when he heard what subject I was studying: "At least you get to eat occasionally!"

"So what's the form here, George? What exactly are we supposed to be guarding the stars' bodies against?"

"Ego deflation," he suggested. "All you do is sit on this unbelievably uncomfortable chair here, outside this locked door here, and count the swirls in the pattern on the puke-coloured carpet here, in this staggeringly featureless corridor."

"This corridor here?"

George nodded. "That's the one. It's easy money, Alan, if you don't bore easily. Only two things you need to know. One, the nearest lavatory is down there." He pointed to the far end of the corridor.

"And two?"

"Two is, if anyone from management come by while you're having a pee and finds your chair empty—you're out. Remember, appearances are everything in this racket. So learn to cross your legs."

"OK," I said. "Sounds simple enough. There much traffic?" I gestured to the door behind which, presumably, the stars lay snoozing. Or whatever it is that stars do in hotel rooms when no-one's watching.

"People come and go every now and then," said George. "And before you ask—no, I didn't recognise anyone. They all wear dark glasses and hats and big coats. Hardly tell men from women, let alone stars from staff."

George left to get some sleep. I settled my bottom onto the chair held vacated, and began counting the swirls in the carpet. I'd reached 143 when, without warning, a heavy weight thudded onto my lap. The only reason I didn't scream and leap into the air was that I'd had all the wind knocked out of me. Some bodyguard.

"Who the hell are you?" I squeaked, my voice strangled by my thumping heart. The largest cat I had ever seen in my life—a gigantic, ginger creature, whose folds of gut hung over the sides of my knees—did not reply. Instead, it settled its bulk more comfortably (for it, not me) and, purring quietly, went to sleep.

This was embarrassing. This was unprofessional. This was extremely uncomfortable.

I tried to shove Ginger off my lap. He didn't resist—he didn't need to resist. His mastery of the rules of gravity meant that I might just as well have tried to shove a sack of potatoes off a table using my nose.

Perhaps if I stood up, the cat would slide onto the swirly carpet? There again, perhaps he would dig his claws in and I'd spend the rest of the night in Casualty receiving blood transfusions.

I couldn't just sit there, though! If someone from management saw me, I'd be sacked for sure. I mean, that's hardly the image the Personal Security Industry tries to cultivate: "Celebrities—Entrust Your Life To A Tall Guy Pinned To A Chair By A Mound Of Ginger Fur!"

Unless, of course, Ginger had every right to be there. He didn't look like my idea of a Hollywood pet—I'd have expected something more slimline, with coiffured whiskers and million-dollar orthodontics—but what did I know? Maybe the Large Look was in for cats that season.

But even if that were the case, it didn't solve my problem. Was I supposed to knock on the door and ask Ms. Quark and/or Mr. Frost whether it was OK for the moggy to come in?

I heard a soft snick behind me, and turned—as far as Ginger's presence allowed—to see a male figure emerge from the stars' suite, dressed in the obligatory dark glasses, hat and big coat.

"Good evening," I said, cold sweat on my brow.

"Good evening," he said, in a deep, North American accent. "You're with the security team, are you?"

"That's right, sir. All quiet out here, so far."

"Good, good." He looked at me, looked at the cat on my lap, looked back at me.

"Yup," I said. "All quiet on the corridor front." Was neither of us going to mention the damn cat? I couldn't stand it any more. "Ah, listen, about the cat . . ."

"Cat?" he said. "Oh yes, this cat here. The ginger one."

"That's the one," I confirmed. "Does it belong to anyone in your party at all? Only, I wasn't quite sure what to do about it."

The American stroked his chin. "Well, I should just carry on as you are doing, I guess. The cat seems happy enough." He carefully and quietly locked the door behind him, nodded to me, and walked off up the corridor towards the lifts.

He hadn't answered my question, I noticed.

This was getting silly: in a moment of impulsive decisiveness which I was to have reason to remember for the rest of my life, I stood up. Just like that: suddenly, in one violent motion. It almost worked, too, but Ginger awoke at the last moment and, exactly as I had feared, plunged his talons into my thighs. There followed a macabre dance, as—trying not to scream out loud—I waltzed up and down the corridor, shaking my legs and batting at the furry behemoth with my hands.

My efforts were frankly ineffectual. Apart from anything, I was restrained by a fear of angering the beast further. Eventually, however, Ginger bored of the game. Pausing only to perform one final act of surgery on my shredded flesh, and to treat me to the filthiest look I'd ever had in my life from anyone, he leapt off and disappeared up the corridor.

I fought to bring my breath back under control, while I inspected the damage. My shirt and trousers were covered with rips and ginger fur, and blood was seeping through here and there. At the very least, I needed to wash out the wounds and sponge off the blood, if I was to make myself look halfway respectable. Despite George's warnings about not deserting my post, I had no choice. I set off at an urgent hobble for the lavatory at the far end of the corridor. I wasn't gone more than five minutes, but as it turned out that was long enough for a significant change to occur to the scene outside the suite door.

My chair was no longer empty. It was occupied by a dead man, with an enormous ginger cat sitting on his lap.

A middle-aged man with a boozer's nose. He'd been garroted. The cat was asleep.

I stared at him for a while, my head spinning, and then I ran down the corridor, down the stairs (I was going too fast to stop for the lift), straight to the night porter's cubby-hole, where a young, balding Sri Lankan chap sat listening to cricket on a portable radio.

I jabbered at him. I panted and gasped. I bled a little from my legs and forearms. I gesticulated and tried not to faint.

I had to wait for a break in play—they take their cricket pretty seriously, these Sri Lankans—but eventually, the porter agreed to accompany me to the fourth floor. When he saw with his own eyes what I'd been talking about, he soon livened up.

"That's the cat!" he said.

"Yes, I know," I said. "And beneath the cat . . ."

"We been looking everywhere for that cat, man! He's not supposed to be upstairs at all!"

"Well," I said, "here he is. But, listen—"

"He's always upstairs, man! That is one very bad cat."

"And a very big cat," I said. "But what about—"

"Not as big as he is bad, believe me. Not nearly." The porter shooed Ginger away with much clapping and hissing: he'd obviously done this kind of work before. "And that," he said, pointing at the corpse, "is Mr. Lynch, the night manager."

"He's dead," I said, trying to inject some urgency into the matter.

The porter shrugged. "He was a drunk and a bully and lazy and he stole."

"Even so, I think we should call the police."

He shrugged again. "Of course. But you know, they have more important things to do with their time."

Life is cheap in the catering trade. That's one lesson they don't teach you at catering college.

I was interviewed at some length by the cops. They were initially excited by my disheveled state, but their excitement turned to derision when they heard about the cat. (Though, to be fair to them, they didn't scoff so loudly once they'd actually met the cat in question). As is their way, they asked a lot more questions than they answered, so most of what I learned about the investigation came from the newspapers. An unreliable source, I know, but for what it's worth, and reading between the lines drawn by Britain's libel laws . . .

O'Quark and Frost, the film stars, were (it was hinted) falling behind in paying for certain of their household utilities—notably, cocaine. A corpse left sitting outside their hotel suite was the underworld equivalent of a red-edged bill.

Just to make sure they got the message about their vulnerability, it was rumoured, a typed note had been left inside the suite itself. The hat-wearing American I'd spoken to was wanted for questioning by both Scotland Yard and the FBI. It was assumed that he was the one who'd broken into the stars' room to leave the note—and probably the one who'd committed the murder, too. My description wasn't much to go on, but the cops seemed confident they'd catch up with him sooner or later—I got the impression they had an idea who he was.

Why kill Lynch, the night manager? That was one question the detectives took an unpleasant delight in answering. "They thought he was you, mate. We reckon he'd had a drink, fancied giving someone a hard time, came upstairs to check on the bodyguard. But you weren't there, so he sat down to wait for you. Drunk as he is, though, he nods off—so when the killer arrives, he sees some bloke snoozing outside the suite, thinks it's one of the bodyguards, and—"

I didn't hear the rest. I was thinking about how close I had come to being randomly garroted. And I was wondering whether Ginger leapt onto Lynch's lap before or after the night manager's death. Could be either, I decided: that cat would sleep through anything. And struggling against an assassin wouldn't be made any easier by the presence across your lap of the Cat of Doom.

One further development caused a flurry of press interest, a week after the murder—the disappearance one night of the aforementioned Cat Of Doom. Well, that's one mystery I can solve. I stole Ginger, and took him home to live with me.

He obviously wasn't being properly looked after at the hotel, and the way I figured it, that cat had saved my life—albeit unintentionally, and indeed painfully. If Ginger hadn't torn my legs to pieces, I'd have been sitting in the death chair when the killer arrived looking for his sacrificial bodyguard.

I put Ginger on a diet, but even so he cost me a fortune in cat food. A little reluctantly, I had to go back to Janet and ask if she'd got any more well paid bodyguarding gigs. She had, and I carried on moonlighting in hotel corridors throughout the rest of my student days. Which is why I am qualified to tell you that bodyguarding—despite what you might read in the papers, and notwithstanding that one memorable night (from which I still have the scars)—is easily the most boring job in the world.

The Bandit Who Caught a Killer

Roman Ranieri

Casey Saunderson glanced up at his lawyer as the thin, wiry man began to pace back and forth in the small conference room.

"Now, Casey, if I'm going to give you the best defense that I can, you have *got* to be honest with me. Did you kill Natalie?"

"No. I didn't kill anybody. I was out of town when she was murdered."

Jerry Chandler stopped pacing in mid-stride and slammed his palm down on the wooden table. "Damn it, Casey! Don't bullshit me! The coroner's report puts the time of death at four to five P.M. Your flight to Toronto didn't take off till six P.M. You *could* have committed the murder."

"But I didn't kill my wife. I still loved her. I wanted her to come back home. You have to prove I didn't do it."

"Wrong, Casey," replied the lawyer, caressing the lapel of his fifteen-hundred-dollar designer suit. "I only have to create *doubt* that you did it. I don't have to prove anything."

Casey smiled. "I guess it's true; you get what you pay for. You and the other lawyers are going to cost me millions by the time this trial is over, but I know you're going to get me off."

Chandler wagged a finger at his client. "Confidence is good, Casey, but don't get cocky. There's a lot of incriminating evidence against you. And some of it will be damn tough to discredit and refute. This trial is going to be a real bitch. Be prepared. The prosecutors will be doing their best to convince the jury that you cold-bloodedly stabbed your wife to death in a jealous rage."

"But I didn't do it."

"Then why did you fly to Toronto? You had no appointment with the people you said you went there to meet. They denied having any knowledge that you were coming until you walked into their office. And when you got back home, why did you make such a spectacle of speeding around town in that purple Ferrari instead of coming straight to the DA's office like I advised you to do?"

"What the hell!" snapped Casey. "Whose side are you on?"

"I'm trying to prepare you for the prosecutors. Their questions will be a lot tougher. It'll be hard to give any answers without incriminating yourself. I want you to be sharp in that courtroom. Always *think* before answering."

"Okay. I understand," said Casey, a sullen expression clouding his face. "I know this isn't going to be easy, but I'm fighting for my life here."

"Don't worry, we're going to do everything we can for you. The main point in our favor is that the police haven't found the murder weapon. A murder conviction is always tougher without a weapon as physical evidence."

"Sounds good. Anything else?"

Chandler opened his expensive designer briefcase, fished out a yellow file folder, and handed it to Casey. "Just study these notes and get plenty of rest tonight. I want you sharp in that courtroom tomorrow."

"You can *bet* on it," replied Casey, flashing his best TV commercial smile.

"That's perfect," Chandler chuckled. "Be sure to save some of that charm for the jury."

The courtroom was packed from floor to ceiling with news reporters and curiosity seekers. The high-profile celebrity status of the defendant made this trial a media circus. Even formerly respectable news networks were battling like rabid dogs for the rights to televise this judicial freak show.

Suddenly, the boisterous crowd was quieted by the booming voice of the bailiff announcing the arrival of the judge. The short, moon-faced man in the black robe smiled and waved hesitantly at the cameras as he took his seat. It seemed that everyone involved in this case had eagerly embraced its sensational aspects.

The trial began with an almost laughable degree of posturing as both sides tried to convince the jury, *along with the TV and radio audiences,* that they and they alone held the key to the truth.

The evidence against Casey was difficult to refute. There had been heated arguments in public places, police reports of domestic disturbances at the Saunderson home, photographs of Natalie's bruised and swollen face. Even several witnesses who testified that they had watched Casey knock his wife to the pavement outside the popular restaurant, Chateau Bistro.

Jerry Chandler took a deep breath, then painted his face with the most ingratiatingly sincere smile that years of dedicated practice could produce, and walked over to the jury. "Ladies and Gentlemen, I agree that the prosecution has shown you that Casey and Natalie did not always enjoy a flawless marriage, but how many of us can boast of constant bliss with our own spouses. Surely all of us have had unpleasant arguments with loved ones. Why, only last night I brought home a dozen red roses to my beautiful wife to make up for some stupid comment I made on the spur of an angry moment." He smiled conspiratorially at the male jurors. "Of course my wife and I really enjoyed making up all night."

The jurors, male and female alike smiled back warmly at Chandler, obviously affected by the cultivated charm radiating from this impeccably groomed man. Although his technical knowledge of the law had been barely adequate enough to pass the bar exam, his sharply honed performance skills were the envy of the entire California legal profession.

The chief prosecutor, Mary Claxon, was an attractive middle-aged woman with a serious, straight-to-the-point demeanor. Although she obviously enjoyed the spotlight as much as the other participants, she refrained from playing to the audience with theatrical gestures and excessive displays of emotion.

Mary paused a moment to take a final glance at her notes, then purposefully strode toward the jury. "Ladies and Gentlemen, in the next several days I will present testimony by a large group of highly-regarded police officers, coroners, forensic scientists, and various independent specialists. When you have heard and considered this amazing collection of facts, you will be unquestionably convinced that Casey Saunderson stalked his estranged wife, Natalie, for several weeks; then coldly and brutally attacked her outside her apartment on the night of February ninth, slashing her throat with such ferocity that he nearly severed her head from her body. Do not allow yourselves to be deceived by this charismatic murderer. Beneath that handsome TV-star face and charming manner is the heart and soul of a blood-thirsty beast."

The trial dragged on for weeks. Each day the outrageous

behavior escalated until only the smallest trace of judicial propriety remained. The pinnacle of absurdity was reached when the prosecution and defense teams confronted each other on a popular TV game show where groups of contestants competed for valuable prizes.

Chandler was literally exhausted after one particularly grueling cross-examination. The witness was an unflappable forensics expert who convincingly testified how it was a ninety percent-probability that some of the blood found at the crime scene belonged to Casey Saunderson. But no matter how incriminating the mounting evidence became, the most powerful asset in Chandler's defensive arsenal was still the absence of a murder weapon. Admittedly, it wasn't much to work with, but Chandler played it masterfully, taunting the police and prosecutors repeatedly with cries of, "Show me the knife" and "If the blade you can't get, you must acquit."

Mary was totally amazed. The jury seemed to be ignoring the virtual mountain of evidence placed before them, and concentrating instead on the absent weapon, and on the few minor procedural mistakes made by the police during the initial investigation. The slimy charms of Casey and Chandler seemed to have the jury members completely enthralled. It was like watching a dozen cobras swaying to the music of two master flutists.

Finally, in a desperate last-ditch tactic, Mary decided to try a change of scenery.

"Your honor, I have recently become convinced that the jury is at a serious disadvantage in their attempt to fully understand the extent of this horrible crime. I respectfully request that they and everyone else involved with this trial be taken out to the murder scene to gain a personal perspective of what took place there."

The judge's round face turned downward in a thoughtful frown. "Would you suggest that we include the news media?" he asked.

"Absolutely, your honor," replied Mary, sensing victory.

"Very well. Do you have any objections, Mr. Chandler?"

"Yes, I do, your honor. I fail to see how this needless field trip will benefit the jury in any way, shape, or form."

"Objection overruled. I want the jury to have access to every possible bit of information concerning this case, regardless of how insignificant it might seem. I intend to do my best to assure that the final ruling of this court is incontestably fair. I will arrange transportation to the crime scene for tomorrow afternoon."

The press corps murmured excitedly. As sensational as this trial was already, they were all hungry for a new twist or angle to exploit. This field trip promised to be ripe with photo opportunities for the afternoon telecasts.

Cold rain fell from a dirty, smoke-gray sky as the four buses pulled up to the curb in the trendy residential neighborhood where Natalie Saunderson had spent the last nine weeks of her tragically short life. As the people began stepping down to the sidewalk, the somber reality of what had occurred here stunned them into silence. Uniformed police officers escorted the group to the section of pavement bordered by tall hedges where the murder had taken place.

The first impression was one of disbelief. How could there possibly be so many bloodstains from only one victim? It was clear to even the most inexperienced observer that the deadly attack had been conducted with a beast-like ferocity and blood lust.

Even though Mary had been here several times before, she still shuddered as she noticed spots of dried blood on the lowest branches of a nearby oak tree. She cleared her throat, then addressed the crowd.

"Ladies and Gentlemen, allow me to draw your attention to the narrow separation between these two hedges on the left. It was here that the murderer crouched in ambush, waiting patiently for a slim, unarmed woman who had no opportunity to defend herself. As she reached this spot, he leaped from his hiding spot and slashed at her throat, his blade slicing cleanly through the neck to the spinal column. Although that first strike was unquestionably a fatal one, he continued to slash and stab at her as her body crumbled helplessly to the walkway."

Chandler became alarmed as he saw the jury's expressions of shock and revulsion changing to anger and determination.

"Your honor, may we proceed into the house now? I would like everyone to see the more than comfortable lifestyle that my client, Casey Saunderson, was providing for his estranged wife even though they were in the midst of a difficult divorce and child custody hearing."

"Very well, Mr. Chandler. Sergeant!" he called to one of the policemen, "We're ready to go inside. Has everything been prepared?"

"Yes, Sir," replied the officer. "We've laid plastic sheeting down on the floors for added protection."

The crowd slowly formed into a single-file line, then quietly and respectfully entered the spacious ground-floor condominium. The furnishings were trendy, but not ostentatiously so. In fact, by southern California's cutting-edge standards, the dwelling was almost spartan.

A short, round Hispanic woman stood silently to one side of the kitchen, regarding everyone with stoic patience as they slowly walked through the house. Mary just happened to glance at the housekeeper as Casey Saunderson entered the kitchen. The woman's facial expression instantly changed to a curious mixture of deference and contempt. She seemed to be acknowledging that he was her boss, yet she had no personal respect for him.

"Hi, Rosie," Casey called out cheerfully. "How's everything?"

"Very fine, Mr. Saunderson," she replied in heavily accented English. "There have been no problems."

"Great, just great, Rosie. You're doing an excellent job."

At that moment, a large white and tan cat entered the kitchen through a pet door near the pantry. It stopped in the center of the room and calmly studied the assembled group of people. When its alert eyes finally came to Casey Saunderson, the creature hissed and bared its fangs defensively.

Casey laughed and looked at the housekeeper. "Bandit has really grown since I was here last. He doesn't even recognize me anymore."

"I think he knows you, Mr. Saunderson," she said.

Chandler, sensing a flare-up of anger from Casey, moved forward to defuse the situation.

"That's a fine animal, Rosie. How old is he?"

"Bandit is two years old. Mrs. Saunderson loved him very much. She used to take him everywhere with her." Rosie's voice suddenly thickened with emotion. "Only that one day she left him at home because he was sleeping when she was ready to go out. If she had waked him, and taken him along, who knows—"

"Shall we go back outside, your honor?" asked Chandler. "I think we're through here."

"Are you in agreement, Ms. Claxon?" said the judge.

"Yes, your honor, let's go."

The news photographers snapped a few final pictures as

the group headed out the front door. As the last person existed, a policeman reached over to pull the door closed. A white and tan blur darted between the officer's legs and ran down the walkway.

Rosie uttered a sharp cry of alarm as she hurried toward the door. "Bandit! Come back here. Bandit!"

The cat ran straight for the crime scene, then stopped suddenly, refusing to step on any of the bloodstains. It quickly scanned the people in the immediate vicinity, then seemed to make a decision and leaped into Mary's arms.

"Hey!" she exclaimed, catching the furry animal. "What do you want, Bandit? I don't have any food for you."

The cat blinked and purred.

"Okay, boy, you can go home now."

But as Mary bent down to release the cat, it dug its claws into the fabric of her blouse and hung on. When she straightened up reflexively, Bandit gracefully shot out of her arms and onto the overhanging branches of the nearby tree.

"Bandit! Bad cat! Get out of that tree!" scolded Rosie as she reached the amused group of people.

Ignoring her, the cat climbed higher until it settled into a narrow depression between two large branches and gazed calmly down at the crowd.

"Come down right now!" yelled Rosie.

"Leave it alone. It'll come down when it's hungry," said one of the jurors.

"No. Bandit cannot stay outside. He grew up in the house. He will become lost out here."

"How can he get lost? He's only about sixty feet from the front door."

Rosie turned to the judge. "Please, your honor, help me get him down. I have grown to love that cat very much."

The judge motioned to the nearest policeman. "Find a

ladder or something and get the cat down."

"Yes, Sir," replied the officer, scowling.

"There is a ladder in the lawn shed in the back yard," said Rosie.

"Okay. Let's go get it."

"Your honor, there's no need to endanger this officer's safety. The cat'll come down by itself," said Casey impatiently.

"The officer is a highly-trained professional, Mr. Saunderson. I'm sure retrieving a cat from a tree will be no problem for him."

The policeman followed the housekeeper around to the fenced back yard and returned a few minutes later with a wooden stepladder.

The cat gazed down, patiently waiting as if the entire scenario was all part of its plan. With an assured economy of motion, the officer carefully placed the ladder at the base of the tree and slowly began his ascent. Bandit made no move.

"Okay, Bandit, just stay right where you are. I'm not going to hurt you."

As the officer climbed closer to the cat, he continued to coax it in a soothing tone of voice. Bandit waited calmly, displaying no fear or aggression. The policeman slowly raised his hand above the cat, then began to pet the animal before attempting to pick it up. The cat blinked and wiggled its ears as the man's gentle hand caressed its furry head.

"Okay. Let's get down now, Bandit."

The officer reached up his other hand and slid it beneath the cat's belly. His fingertips touched something hard and solid under the animal. He lifted Bandit off the object, then peered down into the depression where the cat had been sitting.

"What the hell? I don't freaking believe it!" exclaimed the

officer. "Hey! One of you take this cat and get me an evidence bag," he called down to the other policemen. "We've got the murder weapon up here!"

The officers scrambled as if a bomb had gone off. Within minutes, the policeman who had climbed the ladder, was handing a clear plastic bag to prosecutor Mary Claxon. The bag contained a blood-encrusted hunting knife with a wickedly serrated blade.

"Well, Mr. Chandler. You wanted us to *Show you the knife.* Here it is. Can you see it clearly enough?" she asked, a huge grin brightening her pretty face.

Casey Saunderson moved with the blinding speed he had once used to become one of the world's best Track and Field athletes. The police reacted quickly, but were still left a few steps behind. Reporters screamed at their cameramen to get it all on film as Saunderson reached the street and turned left, with five officers in hot pursuit.

The gap between Casey and the police slowly increased as his long, smooth strides propelled him forward. Casey turned onto a wider street with several meandering pedestrians. The officers had been contemplating firing a few bullets at Saunderson's legs to slow him down, now with innocent bystanders in the vicinity, that was no longer an option. They would have to run him down, or allow him to escape.

An elderly woman with a cane suddenly appeared from the doorway of a gourmet coffee shop. Casey veered at the last moment, but still bumped the woman off-balance.

"Son of a bitch!" exclaimed the woman, reeling backward a few steps. As she glared at Saunderson, her expression of anger changed to one of shocked recognition. She instantly regained her balance and launched her cane at Casey's legs with a spinning motion. The stout wooden projectile struck the running fugitive in the back of his ankles, tangling between his feet as his right foot twisted out from under him.

Casey hit the concrete hard. The air whooshed out of his lungs explosively. He rolled over and desperately tried to get back on his feet. But the police had only needed those few short seconds to close the gap. They pounced on him with trained coordination, slapping the handcuffs on his wrists before he could move an inch.

"That was a hell of a move, lady," said one of the officers, picking up the cane and handing it back to the elderly woman.

"As soon as I got a good look at him, I recognized the son of a bitch," she replied, shaking her fist in the air. "I *knew* that bastard was guilty. I knew he killed her."

"Well, you can help us anytime you like, lady," laughed one of the other policemen.

"I might just do that, junior," she said, nodding smugly.

Back at home, Bandit sat quietly in Rosie's lap, munching one of the tasty treats the woman held in her hand. Certainly, he had no idea that he had just helped convict the killer of his beloved mistress.

Or did he?

Coffee and Murder

Carrie Channell

"Here you are, Sherman dear," said Evelyn Trowbridge to the sleek grey feline on the chair at her side. Despite his thirteen years, Sherman looked like a cat in his prime. He preened as he nipped the morsel from his mistress's fingers.

"Mother, could you please listen?" Jonathan, her eldest, said.

"Mother Evelyn, we're only looking out for your best interests," said Sandra.

"A nursing home is not in my best interest." Sherman raised his head as Evelyn handed him another crumb from her plate. "They won't let me keep Sherman and I won't have my garden."

"It's not a nursing home, mother," said Jonathan. "You can come and go as you please. And you can have a little garden."

"I'm happy here. You just want control of my home and fortune while I waste away in some institution!" Her voice reached such a high pitch the gathered crowd winced. In her rage, Evelyn threw her napkin on her plate. Instantly the butler was at her side, taking the plate.

"Stop!" Evelyn slapped his hand hard. "How dare you, Charles? Sherman isn't finished yet!" Sherman, hearing his name, yawned and stretched.

"I'm sorry, madam," said Charles, quickly withdrawing his hand and rubbing it slightly.

"And don't make a fuss. I didn't hurt you at all," said Evelyn. She sniffed. "Go away. Send out Joanne. She's much more suited to service than you." Charles hurried inside.

"Joanne!" she called. Then louder: "Joanne!"

"Here, madam," she replied, breathing a little heavily as she hurried through the door. She lay a soothing hand on Charles's shoulder as she passed him.

"Take these dishes. They've been sitting here forever!"

"Yes, madam." And the dishes disappeared.

"Mother, why must you be such a pill," said Angelina.

"Speak to me with respect, young lady," snapped Evelyn. She stroked Sherman's head. "Now. Sherman and I are going for a walk in the garden."

Evelyn and I had a lovely walk that day. It was good to see her relax. Her children were such a trial that I began to worry about her heart condition, but she seemed all right. Like all cats, I can read human auras so I could tell if she was doing poorly.

We walked almost to the end of the garden. It stopped abruptly at the property line. Behind that were farm fields and a small access road through them that ended at the back of the garden.

Evelyn sighed in relief when she returned to the cottage to discover her children gone. She remembered for a tiny, tearful moment when they had been just helpless babies. It was almost hard to believe now. She pushed open the door to the back hallway.

"Mother."

Evelyn screeched and clutched her chest. Her heart

109

pounded madly and she fought to control her breathing.

"Frederick. What are you still doing here? Did you misunderstand me?"

"No. But I want to talk with you about another alternative."

Evelyn raised her hand as if to dismiss him again, but paused. Sherman rubbed her ankle and nipped at her feet.

"Stop it, Sherman," she said, pushing the cat away with her foot. "What sort of alternative?"

"We're worried about your health. Don't shake your head, that's the whole of it whether you believe it or not. We love you, Mother, in all your stubbornness. We don't want to wait until you're collapsed without breath on the floor here and can't reach the phone."

Evelyn grimaced.

"You move in with me."

Evelyn laughed.

"Or I'll move in here."

She stopped and leaned close to her youngest son's face. A child could lie to his mother (hadn't Jonathan lied about everything right up to and including that horrid wife, Sandra?) but something in Frederick's look and manner said otherwise.

"Why would you want to live out in the country? The only company is me with my stubbornness and Sherman."

"And Mr. Mortin. Doesn't he still come around to visit?"

"That's none of your business!" she snapped. Then she drew a deep breath. "Well, all right. Yes. He does pay a visit to me from time to time. But why, Frederick?"

Frederick's eyes dropped to the floor. "Things have been . . . difficult for me recently," he said.

"Money?" she asked in a hard voice.

He glared at her. "Yes. But not only that. If it were only

that I would keep at it. I have some, and I have been working."

"A girl, then."

"You could say that."

"So how long before you patch things up or find another, and are on your way back to the city? You want to stay here and recover. If you had come to me and asked me that, perhaps I would have said yes. But to pretend to want to be here to help me when you seek refuge . . . No, Frederick. I deserve more respect than that, and I'm not prepared to upset my lifestyle for your little troubles." She stomped into the front of the house. Frederick gazed after her with hurt and anger in his face for several minutes before slipping quietly out.

I nipped at Evelyn's fingers playfully as she handed me the last morsel off her plate. We finished our meal and moved to the front parlor. Evelyn sat in her favorite chair with a small novel to read and I stretched out before the fireplace to nap when someone pulled the bell. Evelyn started violently.

Joanne answered the door. It was Mr. Mortin. Evelyn looked relieved, I think because it wasn't Frederick, and a little unnerved.

"I'm sorry I didn't call before I came," said Mr. Mortin.

"Well, you did startle me. It's quite unlike you to just drop by, James."

"Yes." He stared around the room, confused. I caught wisps of distress floating around his head. It looked suspiciously like a ghost. We cats can see ghosts all right, but they look like a hundred other ethereal energies, and sometimes I can't be sure.

"James, what is wrong?" demanded Evelyn.

His eyes stopped roving and focused on her suddenly,

completely. The wispy, ghostlike thing disappeared.

"Evelyn, I'm worried about you being here alone."

"You too?" She sat in her chair again and closed her eyes.

"I saw someone outside, on the road. He was staring at your house."

"I'm not alone. Charles and Joanne are here. Really, James, there are people in the country who wander about. Did you even think to go and ask him what he wanted?"

Fully roused, I slipped out of the room and outside through my little door in the kitchen while they continued arguing. I'm not an outside cat, but, like Evelyn, I need my freedom. I saw the figure Mr. Mortin spoke about. He stood in the road, very still. I trotted low to the ground, silently toward him. As I drew closer I realized I wasn't sure whether it was really a man or his imprint. Definitely a man had stood there not long ago. Humans leave imprints of their personalities when they stay in a place, but this one was fading.

I was within ten feet of the figure when I heard a car. It sounded like it was right behind the house, which was strange because I hadn't heard it come down the road. The only ones who knew about the little back road were local farmers, who wouldn't come here, and Evelyn's children. I decided to investigate later and crept closer to the imprint.

At two feet away I stopped. Frederick. It was Frederick, I was sure. But it wasn't recent. He'd stood there all right, and for a long time. It had to be from earlier in the afternoon.

Suddenly there was a slam and a shout. Ducking beside the road, I saw Mr. Mortin storm up the walk and away from the house. At the road he turned in the wrong direction from home; he went in the direction of the will o' the wisp. He barged through the ghostly thing and dispersed the last of the energy. Then I heard the car start and pull away.

Suddenly I felt a chill like nothing I've ever felt before. I hurried back to Evelyn.

"Ouch!" said Inspector Long, sucking at his finger. He glared at the huge grey cat in the chair.

"Sherman!" scolded Joanne. "You must excuse him, Inspector. Since Evelyn's . . . death he's scarcely left her chair and is particularly nasty to everyone. He misses her so." She reached a hand toward the cat who turned away and sniffed. He circled a moment on the chair seat then curled up and gazed at them through half-closed eyes, tail lazily wagging over the edge.

"Have you spoken with everyone, then?" she asked as she served the Inspector coffee. He took a sip and seemed to stare away into nothingness.

Sherman's tail twitched.

"I need to speak to the butler, and then I wish to have everyone here after the reading of the will," he said.

"Yes, of course. Oh, Charles, Inspector Long would like to ask you a few questions," she said as the butler stepped into the room. "Tell me, in your own words, what happened that night," said Long.

Charles glanced once at Joanne.

"We served tea to Mrs. Trowbridge, her two sons, daughter and daughter-in-law. They upset her because they wanted to put her in a home. They all argue all the time. They want control of her money. Anyway, they all left except her youngest son Frederick who was parked behind the garden. He always parks there. He waited in the kitchen for her while she walked in the garden with that beast." He scowled at Sherman who blinked back.

"Later, I retired to the carriage house beside the garden,

113

where I live. Joanne served Mrs. Trowbridge her dinner as usual . . ."

"Stick with what you saw and heard," said Inspector Long.

"Yes. I sat by my window with a beer and some supper and saw a figure in the road. It looked like a man, though it was dark and I couldn't tell for sure. He then moved toward the house, and as he came within the light from the dining room window I recognized Mr. Mortin."

Long nodded slowly.

"A short while later I heard him slam the door and storm off. Just as I was about to go into the house and make sure everything was all right, I heard a car out behind the garden. I hesitated, not wanting to be caught in the middle of a family scene, and then Joanne came in and told me what happened."

"And you remained in your quarters?"

Charles nodded.

He's lying, I thought. I was here that night. The car came before Mr. Mortin left, not after. And he couldn't have known about the figure in the road. He couldn't see it from the carriage house.

I now knew the stranger in the funny hat was here to help find who killed Evelyn. I felt bad about snapping at him. She didn't die of a heart attack like they said at first. I knew that, I could see the pain in her face where she lay. Joanne had been surprisingly calm. She had phoned the doctor.

Strange that Charles didn't come right away when she screamed. Of course, he might not have heard her. The house and carriage house are well built and far from each other. Humans can't hear as well as I can, after all, poor things.

It was already too late when the doctor arrived. I came in soon after and my poor Evelyn lay prone on the floor, her face distorted, the doctor hovering over her. Joanne's already told all this to that fellow in the strange hat.

But she's lying about something. And so is Charles.

"Where did you find her?" said Frederick.

"Here," said Joanne, pointing to the carpet in the living room.

Frederick knelt as the doorbell rang. Joanne hurried to open it.

"My dear, how are you faring?" asked Mr. Mortin as he stepped inside. He stopped abruptly. "You."

Frederick stood. "What are you doing here?"

"Just for some money," said Mr. Mortin, shaking his head.

"Money—why you bastard!" He lunged at Mortin who ducked. Frederick slammed his shoulder against the doorjamb.

"Stop it!" cried Joanne and ran from the room.

"You were the last one to see her alive! I wonder why," said Frederick as he threw a punch. Mortin ducked but caught a glancing blow in the chest. He swung back and knocked the younger man to the floor.

"How dare you. I came here to propose to your mother!"

"That's enough of that!" Charles strode into the room and separated them.

No one noticed me when I slipped into the room. They were too busy settling their own loud quarrel. Tempers have been flaring lately, not the least mine. I crept between Mr. Mortin's feet and rubbed his leg quickly. He started and nearly stepped on my tail, but I found out what I wanted to know. Frederick gazed at me with a strange look on his face, but then bent over and rubbed my head.

"Mother," he whispered.

Evelyn, I thought and meowed loudly at him. The door opened and Angelina came in.

"Well, well," said Frederick. "You know, Inspector Long has been asking all of us where you've been."

Angelina tossed her hat onto Evelyn's favorite chair. Sherman immediately leapt up and knocked it to the floor. Angelina swiped at him but he ducked under the chair after one scratch across the crown, ruining the hat.

"Little bastard."

"Where have you been?"

"None of your business." She looked from Mr. Mortin to Joanne to Charles. Frederick motioned to them and they left the room.

"I've spoken with Inspector Long," said Angelina.

"Did you tell him you borrowed my car?"

"Of course not! He didn't ask, so I didn't volunteer." She turned and nearly tripped over Sherman. "Get away from me, you beast!"

This last remark was aimed at me. I'd rubbed her leg with my head and she kicked at me. I almost got away, but she bruised my side a little with her high heel. But I got what I wanted.

Angelina didn't do it, either. She was here that night, it shows in her nervousness. But she didn't come in. She wanted to talk to Evelyn one last time, but she chickened out.

Inspector Long tapped a pencil against his temple. Everyone watched him. The will was read and each offspring had received a comfortable amount, but a large cut of the long-term investments as well as the house and land were bequeathed to Joanne, the maid. They were all still in a state of shock and no one met Joanne's gaze. Long hoped to take advantage of the situation. Too many suspects, too many motives. As of yet no one had given theirself away.

His gaze strayed to the grey cat in front of the fireplace. His brow furrowed. The cat stared back at him unblinking. His tail twitched once.

Where was the cat that night? he wondered. For some reason, he couldn't tear his gaze away.

He stepped to Angelina's chair and placed a hand on the back of it. The cat licked its paw and yawned.

This is ridiculous, thought Long. The cat can't know anything.

Sherman dropped his paw and stared at Long, his eyes half-closed and angry.

The Inspector knew I could tell. His aura showed it clearly, but he denied it. He didn't want to believe it. It reminded me how much I missed Evelyn.

"Thank you," said Inspector Long as Charles brought coffee. Joanne poured as he quietly stepped around the room handing out cups. As he passed Evelyn's chair, Sherman hissed loudly. He swatted at Sherman to get off. Losing his balance he tipped and spilled the coffee onto the chair and the cat. Sherman screeched and leapt straight up in the air, landing on Charles's shoulder.

"Get off!" he cried, pulling at the cat. But Sherman dug his claws in and held tight.

Why didn't I see it before? I felt it the instant I landed on him, just like a shot through my middle, cold, like the moment Evelyn died. He poisoned her. His guilt raged off him like cold, white fire. I dug in and tried to tear him to shreds. My grief engulfed me, as it hadn't since that dreadful night.

117

★ ★ ★ ★ ★

Long pulled at the cat, shouting at Charles to be quiet. Everyone was in turmoil as Long ripped the cat away, trailing shreds of bloody cloth.

"Bastard! I should've killed you, too!" cried Charles, his face red with rage and pain.

The room fell silent.

I heard Evelyn's soft laugh above me when they finally quieted. I curled in Inspector Long's arms as he said: "Would you care to explain that comment?"

Charles glanced at Joanne, who had collapsed in tears at the dining room table. It took a long time, but the gist of it was that Charles and Joanne wanted to marry and move away, but they couldn't on the stipend Evelyn paid them. Part of their pay was room and board, so they couldn't leave. Charles hated Evelyn and convinced Joanne that hastening her death would save everyone years of pain. Joanne had almost backed out, but then so many angry people were there that day and night, that Charles decided to do it. After all, anyone could get blamed for it.

I sat in Inspector Long's lap. He idly stroked my back. We looked at each other knowingly. I think Evelyn would have liked him.

Catabolism

Edo van Belkom

Detective Joe Williams had ended his shift and was ready to leave for the day when a young blonde-haired woman stepped up to his desk and cleared her throat.

"Can I help you?" asked Joe.

"Is this where I report a missing person?" She was an attractive woman, sexy enough to be a dancer, but looking a little ragged—as if she hadn't been getting much sleep the past few days.

Joe sighed and nodded. He worked homicide, but had been handling missing persons while Maguire was away on his honeymoon. He'd almost made it through the week without a single report being filed, and now he had one come in right at the end of the day. "Who's missing?"

She sat down. "My boyfriend."

"He have a name?"

"Danny," she said, clearly reluctant to give him the information. "Danny Lowinger."

The name sounded familiar. Danny Lowinger . . . "I think I arrested him once?"

"Probably," she said softly, her eyes sweeping the floor. "He's been in jail a few times."

It was starting to come back to Joe. Danny Lowinger was a career small-timer who made his living ripping off homes and businesses after hours—the sort of guy they used to call a cat burglar. Joe had caught him robbing a stereo store about ten years back when Joe had still been walking a beat.

"I think I remember him now. Short, stocky guy with thick black hair, and a mole right here." Joe touched his cheek.

"That's him," she said.

"Why do you think he's missing?"

"I haven't seen him in days."

"That unusual for him?" Joe asked, knowing that people in Danny's line of work often disappeared for a while before resurfacing with a pocketful of cash.

"No," she shook her head. "I mean, he's been gone before, but no matter where he went, he always called to let me know he was all right."

"And he didn't call this time?"

She shook her head and sniffed back a tear.

Joe placed a box of tissues on the desk in front of her and she took one. He watched her a few seconds unable to decide if she was putting on an act or not. It was possible that she was filing a missing persons report to start the ball rolling on some insurance scam. Then again, she did seem to be pretty shaken up. Maybe this was all on the level.

"Do you know where Danny was heading the night he went missing?" Joe knew this was a question she probably wouldn't answer since it would place Danny at the scene of some crime. But instead of playing dumb, she nodded.

"Where?"

She took a deep breath, then hesitated a moment, as if deciding how to answer the question. Joe gave her all the time she needed. After all, she was about to finger her boyfriend for some job, and that would either put him back in jail or end their relationship—probably both.

"1534 Dorchester Avenue."

"You sure?" asked Joe. He wouldn't put it past her to give him a phony address just to get him looking for Danny.

"He found out from a travel agent friend of his that the family would be in Mexico for two weeks. They got back last Friday."

All of Joe's skepticism suddenly vanished. Obviously Danny Lowinger was missing, and judging by the way this woman was providing information, she was afraid something bad might have happened to him. Given the nature of Danny's occupation, Joe was inclined to agree with her. "Well, Miss uh . . ."

"Crystal," she said. "Crystal Shard."

"Well, Miss . . . Shard, if you fill out this form," he placed a pad of paper on the desk next to the box of tissues, "I'll do my best to find him."

"Thank you." She began writing.

The next morning Joe searched the files for a report of a robbery at 1534 Dorchester Avenue. He found one filed on Saturday the 14th, the day after the family had returned from their Mexico vacation. Obviously, Danny had broken into the house and gotten away with the loot.

But as Joe read on, it became apparent that he hadn't gotten far.

The following Monday all of the items reported stolen were returned by someone named Mavis Mallick who lives at 1526 Dorchester Avenue. Mavis Mallick, thought Joe. For some reason, that name was familiar to him too.

According to the report, Ms. Mallick discovered the stolen items in her backyard and held onto them until she brought them to the police Monday morning.

Very neighborly of her, thought Joe, but something about it wasn't right. If the woman found a VCR and a bag of jewelry out in her backyard, why didn't she call the police right away so they could examine the scene?

He ran a check on Ms. Mallick and it started to make sense. Mavis Mallick was a local crazy who'd been called "The Cat Lady" in the local paper because she had close to twenty cats living in her house. With so many cats, and living on a fixed income, she sometimes had trouble feeding them all, which had attracted the attention of neighbors and eventually the local chapter of the SPCA.

Eventually, city councilors were forced to create a by-law restricting the number of pets in a home within the city limits to four. But, since Ms. Mallick had plenty of public support of her own, the council couldn't force her to get rid of any of her cats. In the end, she and others like her were given exemptions that allowed them to keep their current number of pets, but which prohibited them from acquiring any more. Ms. Mallick must have brought the stolen property to the station so the police wouldn't have had to come to her house and count her cats. With that many cats around, it was conceivable that she'd had a few additions to the brood of late.

So, one mystery solved, another remained.

Obviously Danny had gotten out of 1534 Dorchester with the goods and made it as far as 1526, just four houses away. There, he either vanished into thin air, or something happened that caused him to leave the loot behind.

And considering Danny made his living robbing people's homes, it must have been something bad to make him drop everything and run.

Joe decided to pay Ms. Mallick a visit.

Dorchester was a fairly busy street with a car coming by every few minutes, even in the middle of the day. The same would likely be true in the evenings since it was connected to a major roadway at each end. Joe drove around the block and found that a long alleyway ran behind the houses on the north side of Dorchester. The alley served as a driveway for the rows of garages belonging to the apartments on Keele Street just a bit further north. So in the middle of the night, the alley provided an ideal way to get to a house on Dorchester.

Joe parked his car in the alley and searched for number 1534. He recognized the house's beige bricks and Tudor-styled upper floor and envisioned Danny breaking in through one of its rear basement windows.

Sure enough, one of the basement windows was still boarded up with a sheet of plywood.

That meant that Danny had come out through the back-yard and headed west, probably back to his car. Joe retraced the man's steps slowly, searching the ground and sur-rounding area for anything out of the ordinary.

Four houses over, he came upon number 1526. There were two cats in the backyard, both looking at him curiously as they licked their chops the way cats always do after a big meal.

He stopped in the alley a moment and looked over the house. It was as big as the others on the block, but not nearly as well maintained. There was paint peeling off the wood siding, a few window screens torn out and junk piled up in one corner of the yard. It sure didn't look like a home that would attract a professional burglar.

Except . . .

Except the back door was open to let the cats in and out of the house as they pleased. And at night, it would be hard to tell that the house was run down. At night, the house would simply look like easy pickings to someone like Danny Lowinger.

Maybe Danny had pressed his luck.

Joe was about to hop the fence and take a look around the back yard when he noticed something about the top cross-piece—it was damaged. A long, wide sliver of it had been torn away leaving the fresh wood exposed, in sharp contrast to the white paint covering the rest of the fence.

Joe ran his finger over the painted part of the crosspiece, and imagined it could get pretty slippery with condensation on a cool night like they'd been having of late.

A scenario began to form in Joe's mind.

Danny robs 1534 and heads back to his car with the loot. On the way he sees the back door to 1526 wide open and decides to put in a little overtime. As he's climbing the fence he slips and falls—maybe breaking a leg, maybe breaking his neck.

So far so good.

But, what happened to the body?

Perhaps Ms. Mallick knew.

Joe got back into his car, drove around onto Dorchester and pulled in the driveway at 1526. There were a couple of cats sitting on the porch, drinking in the morning sun and looking like picture postcards of contentment. He stepped up onto the porch and rang the doorbell. After a brief wait, he knocked on the door.

"Just a minute," came a voice from inside.

A few moments later, the door opened and Joe was struck by a gust of fetid air as it rushed to get out of the house.

"Mavis Mallick?" he said, breathing through his mouth.

"Yes?" She smiled at him like a doting grandmother. Her clothes were worn and tattered, but not dirty. Judging by the faded colors of her blouse and pants, they'd been washed hundreds of times before.

"I'm Detective Joe Williams—"

"Hello," she said with a nod. "I already brought the stolen property to the police."

"I know that, ma'am," said Joe. "But I need to ask you a few questions about how you came to find the goods in your backyard."

"I looked out my kitchen window and there they were." She began to close the door. "Bye now."

Joe stuck his foot in the doorway. "That's not all I needed to know," he said. "Mind if I come in?"

"Why, no . . . I, uh . . ."

He pushed the door open and stepped past her into the house.

Inside the smell didn't seem so bad. Or maybe it was that his nose was getting used to the stink, which he decided was either cat poop or rotting food. The interior of the house looked old and every bit as run down as the outside had been. Surprisingly though, it was pretty clean considering how many cats were about. The place was decorated in a busy country decor with plenty of old stuff hung up on the walls and bric-a-brac everywhere else. If he had to describe it in a word, Joe would have said it looked comfortable. That certainly seemed to be the opinion of the cats that were lying around—six in the living room alone—making the count ten so far. Joe didn't care all that much about the cats—they all looked to be well fed and cared for, and probably provided some comfort to the old woman in her waning years. Still, there sure were a lot of them hanging around . . .

"According to the police report I read, you found a VCR and a bag full of jewelry and other items in your backyard."

"That's right." She stood in the middle of the living room, placing herself between Joe and the kitchen. "I brought them to the police because I didn't want any trouble. Not everyone cares about cats as much as I do."

"Of course," said Joe absently. "But I'd like to know if you found anything else out there?"

"Anything else? Like what?"

"Well, to be honest, I was wondering what happened to the man who stole the items that you returned to the police. You didn't, by any chance, find him in your backyard too, did you?"

"No." She said the word quickly, then looked away from Joe at one of her cats.

It wasn't much of a gesture, but it was enough to tell Joe he was onto something. "Because," he continued as if she hadn't denied a thing, "it's pretty strange for someone to rob your neighbor's house, dump the stuff in your backyard and then never be heard from again."

"He's missing?" she said with exaggerated surprise. "I wouldn't think someone would miss a common thief and house robber."

It was an odd thing to say. Joe studied her a moment, and decided to be wary of the old woman. "You wouldn't think so, but someone does miss him very much."

"Well, I wonder what could have happened to him?" She pulled her lips back in something that was a poor imitation of a smile.

"You know what I think happened?"

"No, what?"

"I think he robbed your neighbor's house and was on his way home when he noticed your back door open and decided to take a look around. When he climbed the fence, he slipped and fell, hurting himself bad. Real bad."

She hesitated a moment, then shook her head. "I already told you, I didn't find anyone in my backyard." She was still smiling, but her eyes were darting around now from cat to cat as if she were looking for something that was lost.

Joe glanced at each of the cats nearby, watching them all smack their lips as if they'd just been chowing down on some prime rib.

And that's when it hit Joe in the gut, a thought so sickening it made his stomach churn. Danny Lowinger had made it into the house, but he'd never left.

Joe didn't want to believe it. Mavis Mallick didn't look much like a killer, but there was something about her—something not right in her eyes—that made Joe uneasy. Who knew what she might be capable of, especially when it came to her cats?

"You know," he said, stepping toward the kitchen and sniffing quietly. The bad smell seemed to be coming from in there. "You have a lot of cats, Ms. Mallick."

"Twenty," she said, trying to block his way.

"Twenty, right. I would think they cost you an arm and a leg to feed."

"I would never let them go hungry."

"Oh, I can see that." He glanced over her shoulder into the kitchen. There was a litter box there, but it was clean. Obviously that wasn't the source of the bad smell. But there was a bowl of moist cat food next to the litter box and that was heaped full. Joe moved past her into the kitchen. He stepped closer to the bowl, sniffed at it, and found the source of the stink. He turned to her and said, "They all look like they've been eating well."

She glanced at the refrigerator. "I take care of them as best I can."

Joe noticed the darting look in her eyes and wondered why she didn't just tell him not to look into the refrigerator. Now he had to look inside it, even though he had a sickening feeling that he wouldn't like what he would find.

"You have something to drink?" he asked.

"Water," she said, quickly moving to the kitchen sink and getting a glass out of the cupboard.

"No, I was thinking of something else." He walked over to the refrigerator. "You know . . . maybe some milk"—and grabbed the handle.

"No!"

He pulled open the refrigerator door . . . and felt his stomach begin to spasm.

Danny Lowinger wasn't a missing person any more.

However, there were several pieces of him missing.

Impressions

Janet Pack

"Sorry to call you in on your day off, Sergeant. We need your help."

The young detective tried not to smile as Rob Magnin struggled up the narrow steps of the apartment house, one large cat carrier in each hand.

"Just got back from the vet," he puffed, thinking he needed more Stairmaster work at the gym and squinting green eyes at the open and yellow-taped door of the crime scene. "Too cold to leave my friends outside, so I'll tuck 'em inside here. Hope no one's allergic."

"Just West. He left a few minutes ago."

After stowing his pets safely and draping his coat over the top of their plastic prisons, Detective Sergeant Magnin walked through the apartment in search of the officer in charge. He found Higgins in the kitchen resting a substantial hip against the sink and slowly shaking his head. "We've been all over this place for the last couple hours, Sergeant," the balding man greeted. "Can't find anythin' except the resident's own prints." He consulted a small notebook. "Name, Fran Lloyd. White, middle-aged, an English Lit perfesser at the college a couple miles from here. Quiet, seldom has anyone in. No pets. One parkin' ticket, otherwise a perfect drivin' record. Her car, a gray Chevy Cavalier, is in the carport behind the apartment, and shows nothin' unusual.

"Call to 911 came in this mornin'. One of her neighbors heard an awful commotion from this apartment and reported it. He also got part of it on tape." Higgins produced the cassette from his jacket's right side pocket and handed it to Rob. "The neighbor called again, real worried when there wasn't a sound from here after the fight. We arrived twenty minutes later—nothin' was out of place 'cept two breakfast dishes in the sink. Didn't eat all of her bran flakes and raisins. Starbucks coffee in the pot, still warm. But no perfesser. She didn't have a heart attack joggin', didn't fall asleep at the nearest bagel place, didn't have an accident and scoot to the Emergency Care center. Checked all the hospitals, too. We've been through the neighborhood for ten blocks on each side. Everything in the refrigerator's even been sampled and sent to the lab for poison testing. We tapped the walls, the ceilin', and the floors for trap doors. Nothin'."

Magnin scratched his short ginger-colored mustache, a habit when he was puzzled or thinking. "Must've missed something somewhere."

"Yeah, and I'm on overtime," Higgins replied, leading them to the hallway. He spotted the carriers next to the door. "You got new partners?"

"Just had their yearly shots. It never makes Syd or Mayhem sleepy like others I've heard about. I didn't want to leave them out in the cold."

"Well, I'm going to check in at the station, then go home and hit the pillow." Higgins yawned, showing all his fillings. "Long night. Luck."

"Thanks." Rob turned to a passing detective with a camera. "Brunelli, did you—"

One of the cats wailed, a sound long and painful, as if

130

someone were pulling her inside-out by her plumy question-mark tail.

"Mayhem!" Magnin leaped toward her, opening the welded wire door and lifting out one of his best friends. Cuddling her long body against his chest, he checked her legs, her belly, her torso, her head. "What's wrong, girl?" he murmured into her satiny fur. "What's the matter? Those shots finally get to you?"

Mayhem turned wide golden-green eyes on her human friend, then kicked suddenly against his chest with all four feet. Unhurt but surprised, the detective let go. The feline arced and twisted, landing just beyond his reach on the Kilim-copy area rug with tail at attention, eyes like full moons, nose lifted, the edges of its commas moving with each breath. She uttered the peculiar wail again, this time echoed by Syd from his carrier.

"Hey, Sergeant, your cat's—"

"I know," Magnin snapped, intrigued by Mayhem's peculiar behavior. "Everybody shut up. Boy, the captain's gonna have a fit about this." Reaching behind him, he thumbed the latch on Syd's container. The black cat with dark amber eyes and a white cameo on his chest pounced out and, all senses alert, followed his companion.

The cats paced one after the other down the hallway and stopped between the kitchen and the second bedroom, which the professor had turned into a library-study. Slowly Syd rose to his back feet, placed his paws against the kitchen entryway, and stretched as high as he could reach. With a dissatisfied snort, he returned to all fours and led the way into the other room.

Crammed six-foot high bookshelves lined nearly all of three walls, barely leaving space for the door and the single window. A simple oak desk sat to one side, crowned with a computer, a stack of hardbacks, and a green banker's light. The utilitarian gray secretarial chair sat behind. A comfortable wing chair, upholstered with a print Magnin thought must be a Victorian reproduction, sat with one shoulder in daylight, the other attended by a brass swing-arm reading lamp.

Mayhem went straight for the books, standing on her back feet and reaching as high as she could with declawed front paws. She targeted one book repeatedly. Magnin looked. "Shakespeare, *Love's Labour's Lost*," he read aloud. It sat among a number of other works by English playwrights, all in matching blue bindings with gold lettering. "Did Higgins search these books?" he asked a passing detective.

The young man shook his head. "They're so jammed in there, obviously not disturbed, he only had the spines dusted. Like with the rest of this place, we found nothing unusual."

"Okay. Give me your gloves." Carefully Rob pulled on the plastic covers and drew out the book she'd indicated as Mayhem danced around his ankles, butting his calves encouragingly with her head and tail. He held the volume up by the spine and shook it. Nothing. Flipping it over, he allowed the book to open in his hands.

Carefully placed between the pages was a picture of a man and a woman in clothes popular about ten years ago. They stood beside a green Jaguar sedan, their arms around each other.

"Bag!" Magnin called. If not for Mayhem, they might never have found the photo. And he'd bet it had bearing on the case. The young policeman scrambled to offer his sergeant a plastic evidence envelope. Rob upended the book, making the picture slide into its new haven. "Get that to the station pronto, along with this." As he slid the tome into another bag, a worm of suspicion wriggled in his brain. The man in the picture looked familiar. "Dust it first, then send it to the FBI and ask for identifications, specifically in their Witness Protection Program."

Another yowl sailed upscale. Magnin jumped and turned. "Syd! What's wrong?"

The amber-eyed black cat pawed at the window as if desperate to get into the wan sunlight. The sergeant, followed closely by Mayhem, stepped across the room and looked beyond the glass.

The aperture sat above an alley just wide enough for two cars to pass, leading to the carport. The window was a copy of another set in a twin building of the apartment complex across the driveway.

"I don't see anything suspicious," the detective stated to the cat. Mayhem joined her companion, paws on the window, her round eyes turned on her human. Reading his soul, connecting him to . . . to something, he wasn't sure what.

Opening the tilt-out pane, he felt carefully beneath the sill. Just under the overhang his searching fingers probed a regular dent. Something cracked against his fingers. He lifted them, finding barely-dry paint nearly matching the off-white of the upper stories.

Camouflaged. Could the dent have been made by a hook or an eyepin recently screwed into the wall?

"Go to the next building and check out the apartment across from this one," he snapped. "See who last rented it and when. Dust the whole place for fingerprints. Feel beneath the outside of that windowsill and discover whether there's another dimple like the one I just found. I want answers, NOW!"

Four men left to do his bidding. Shortly after Rob had captured and secured his buddies in their cat carriers, he pulled some of the answers from the complex's supervisor. Nervous, the young woman had been questioned earlier by Higgins, felt she'd done a good job answering, and was bothered by Magnin's insistence on going over the same details.

Two young professional males had rented the apartment, but stayed only three months even though they signed a year's lease. They'd moved out a week ago, left no forwarding address. She'd only now gotten the cleaning crew scheduled. As the sergeant released the supervisor with thanks, Magnin's team reported in. They lifted no fingerprints except a very smudged unreadable pair, and there was indeed another uneven spot under one bedroom windowsill, filled and painted like the one Magnin had found.

Now he had to wait for lab results. Working his way back down the narrow stair with the cat carriers, the detective sergeant resigned himself to personal frustration until he learned what had happened to Fran Lloyd. He'd also have to face the ire of his captain tomorrow: first for letting his cats out at a crime scene, the second for following up the clues found by the felines that set his department on the right track toward solving a difficult case. Placing the carriers in his car's back seat, he wondered idly if he couldn't get Syd and Mayhem deputized. Even that probably wouldn't make a difference.

Rob's meeting with the captain came first the next morning. He felt flayed afterward. Then FBI Special Agent Ruth Gibbs appeared at Rob's desk. She asked for privacy. They settled in a small conference room with coffee, sitting across the battered table from each other.

"Fran Lloyd was in our Witness Protection Program," Gibbs began. "We're very upset they found her. She was buried pretty deep, but she's the type that likes stability. The last time we suggested she move, she refused."

"Mob connections?" asked Magnin.

"Right," the agent nodded. "At one time, Lloyd was a girl-friend of the man in the picture, 'Gentleman George' Furillo. He controlled most of the Northeast rackets, money laun-dering, drugs, prostitution, you name it. A powerful guy. She turned in evidence against him after a violent argument which caused them to end their relationship. He had already tried to kill her twice. Lloyd came to us for protection. Her testimony put him and a bunch of his henchmen away for a long time.

"Those two men who rented the other apartment are real pros despite being young. You'll probably never find the body. Any speculations how they did it?"

Rob nodded. "The weapon had to be small, perhaps a long-bladed scalpel, letting most of the damage to be inflicted inside with little blood loss. Those dimples we found under the windows were for hooks. They could have put those up at night, or dressed as maintenance men. I'll bet they kept copies of their apartment keys so they could get back in after convincing the supervisor they'd abandoned the place. The alley was seldom used during the day—unless a neighbor hap-pened to be looking out a window after the murder, no one would see a man sling a waterproof garment bag or some such on a wire and scoot it across to his partner in the other build-ing. That took only a couple of minutes. I assume she was still relatively small, so pulling her in through the second window wouldn't have been difficult. Then they cut off the wire, dis-posed of her body, and came back later to remove the hooks."

Special Agent Gibbs smiled a little. The expression bright-ened her face and made her good-looking, the sergeant thought to himself.

"I heard your cats had something to do with finding clues."

Embarrassed, Rob looked into his coffee, then up again. "Yeah."

Her smile widened as she stood and pulled a business card from her tailored jacket pocket, dropping it on the table. "My friend is starting a research project at the university. It deals with cats reacting to strong human emotions tied with objects or places. She says felines are especially sensitive to that sort of thing, the same impressions psychics sometimes pick up. Apparently, cats do it every time. It's what makes them try to climb blank walls acting like they want to get at an object only they can see, or stare into nothing and yowl." The agent turned to leave. "I've told her you'll be in touch."

"Yeah," Magnin said, reaching for the card and escorting her to the door. "Yeah, I just might."

Diamond Mozzarella

Tom Piccirilli

The Capeesh, in his ratty robe and smelling of bad *pesto funghi*, had been doing this kind of thing with the cat for about six weeks now, and I could tell that Nicky Francesci was about to crack any day. Mama Capesci was upstairs saying her novenas, dressed in black and wearing the little hat with the veil, having knocked back two bottles of wine with lunch. She could really swing with the prayers when she'd put some vino away, and by three o'clock she was having a party with Saint Francis and Saint Anthony, listening to her Jerry Vale records at full volume.

In the old days my father had been Don Capesci's chief enforcer, and I'd more or less inherited the position when my Dad got smeared by a Brownie troop on rollerblades when he crossed against the red at Columbus Circle. The trouble was that, except for my occasionally strong-arming the Chinese delivery kid when he forgot the extra soy sauce, there hadn't ever been much for me to do since I came on board.

Finally giving in to Alzheimer's at the age of seventy-eight, and with a couple of .32 slugs in his temporal lobe since 1956—when the Fratelli sisters broadsided him outside of Steinberg's bakery—the Capeesh had held strong through the roughest times the Family had ever seen. He'd gotten into and out of bed with the unions, staved off J. Edgar's crackdown in the 60s, survived two hits put out on him from rival

Mafiosi, and once played golf with Castro in Havana. Now, when almost all the business was legal and his fortune had been packed away into offshore holdings and retail outlets, he'd suddenly put together a rough crew and started kicking over jewelry stores, just so he could drape his cat in diamonds.

The new crew was run by a two-time loser named Delgatto who'd already nearly gotten pinched again a week ago, after the last heist. He'd been in the stir about half his life and still got a little maudlin whenever he talked about C-Block. The advice he took on the inside had made him an even worse heist-man—he never realized the irony of taking suggestions from other burglars who were also in the pen. His time at Rykers had given him a real attitude, and he must've practiced curling his lip by watching Elvis movies, especially *Charro*. His crew consisted of three other ex-cons from C-Block —all named Billy—who liked to consider themselves cat burglars even though they each weighed about three hundred and were still putting more on thanks to Mama's baked *mostaccioli* and *tortellini alfredo*.

Delgatto and the Billys wore arsenals of Glocks and Brownings and Desert Eagles, and each of them kept a .22 down in an ankle holster. They had a nice hard laugh, coming way up from the bottom of their rotund bellies, when they learned I didn't carry a gun.

Nicky Francesi started going to confession again. We could all feel the heat already building as the articles about the thefts moved up on to page three, but the crew didn't care much since the Capeesh let them keep the gold, silver and jewels, so long as they turned the diamonds over to him and his cat.

The cat was named Mostriciattolo, which meant "little monster," but Neapolitans always bastardized the Italian language and everybody just started calling him Mozzarella, or Mozzy, for short.

Theresa, the Capeesh's twenty-year-old granddaughter, was spending her college break here in the city and looked about as bored as I used to on summer break. Of course, I didn't have a horse ranch, the entire seventeenth floor at the Waldorf, or floor seats to the Knicks, so the parallel sort of stopped short. She also had the better part of the slick goombas in Brooklyn, the artistes in the East Village, and the high financiers on Wall Street sending her everything from Freightliner's filled with white roses to Pontiac Sunfire Sport Coupes to suicidal poems scratched into the wet labels on bottles of Dewars.

She was still bored, and it made my heart tug to the left when I looked at her in the living room with her black curls drifting into her dark and eternal eyes, the angles of her body shown off to perfection as she lay on the couch, her blouse open one button too far, skirt up to give a tantalizing view of what I already knew so well, as she stared me down. Considering how beautiful she was, and how low a tolerance for inactivity she had, I wound up with a seriously bad feeling in my guts.

Mozzarella, currently worth about 2.5 million with a five carat intense blue pear-shaped diamond solitaire choker around his neck, purred as he brushed up and down my legs. Nicky Francesci chewed his lips until they were white, grimacing at Mozzy. He'd been the consigliere for the Capesci family for almost forty years, and it was clear this thing with the cat had pushed him to the edge. We sat in the parlor looking up the corridor at the kitchen, where the Capeesh was gumming his breakfast. It was four in the afternoon. Nicky watched the calico twine against me, and whispered, "This is bad, Joseph."

"I know."

"We finally get in the clear and now we got bugs on the phones again and all kinds of surveillance. They got satellites can count your nose hairs, can you imagine how they're gonna like seeing a cat strutting around in stolen Cartiers?"

I thought he'd meant it was bad about Theresa being bored, but the Feds jumping on us again wasn't any too sweet either.

Nicky shook his head and tried to quit chewing his lips but he couldn't quite stop. "Goddamn Capeesh doesn't even close the drapes."

Mozzarella walked up the hallway and jumped into the old man's lap. The Capeesh sucked some more of his toast, absently stroked the cat, and stared straight ahead. He grunted, and after a couple minutes grunted again. After a while I realized he was calling my name. I went to him and listened closely. He said, "Joseph, I don't think he's giving it all to me."

"Who, Don Capesci?"

"Delgatto."

"All the ice?"

"He smiles too much."

I agreed with that. For a guy who got dreamy about C-Block, Delgatto went around through life looking way too happy with himself. Nicky slinked up behind me and swallowed loudly a few times. Theresa drifted in as well and grinned until her dimples were once again doing to me what they did to every other man who still had a pulse.

"The next heist is tomorrow night," Capeesh said. "You go with them, Joseph."

"Me, Don Capesci?"

"Make sure they're turning over what they should."

"Me, Don Capesci?"

He turned in his seat and shot me one of those glares that

forty years ago would have sent most of Little Italy running for Staten Island. He still had it, sometimes. When he stared at you like that it looked like the two bullets the Fratelli sisters had put in his skull had crawled through his head to sit in his eye sockets. "Did you hear me, Joseph?"

"Yes."

"And take Mozzy. Let him pick out something special for himself. Whatever he wants, you make sure you get it for him."

I shot an imploring glance over to Nicky but he ignored me pretty well, still eating his lips. I wondered, if I turned stoolie, if the Feds would set me up someplace where I could still get good *pasta fagoli* and didn't have to spend my Saturday nights bowling with the elk club. Probably not.

"Sure, Don Capesci," I said.

Theresa stepped in and I saw the excitement writhing in her eyes. I knew it wasn't because she fancied marrying me and getting into the Witness Protection Program and moving to Idaho. "Nonno," she said to her grandfather, bringing her dimples out in full. "Nonno, let me go on the job, too. I'll keep Mozzy safe and keep an eye on everyone and make sure nothing goes wrong."

A minute ago the Capeesh still had the old sharpness for a second, and I prayed that if he had any tightened screws left, a couple-cards in the deck, he wouldn't let her go along. Nicky sat up straight and made a face like a baby with diaper rash might make, but no sounds came loose. I figured I looked sort of the same way. Theresa smiled some more and my chest grew warm, and Mozzarella cocked his head at me.

"Okay, honey," the Capeesh said, his mouth full of wet toast because he'd forgotten to swallow it. "But dress warm."

Jerry Vale got louder and louder, while Mama trundled upstairs and guffawed drunkenly with the saints.

Delgatto had picked a family jewelry shop over on Canal Street, in the heart of the downtown jewelry district. I had to admit it was good choice because it was a small place without any high-tech alarm work. Right next door—completely out of place on the block—was a bookstore apparently devoted to classic American literature. Delgatto and the Billys planned on cutting through the wall of the bookstore and then more or less doing a smash and grab once they were inside the jewelry shop. It was the kind of plan dumb enough to work once or twice, but by now the crew was really pushing their luck. The most sophisticated burglary tool they carried was a sledge-hammer.

When Delgatto used the boltcutters to cut the lock and lift the draw gate to the bookstore, Theresa let out such an "Oooh!" of impressed delight that he actually blushed in the moonlight. The Billys made a hell of an effort to act tough walking up the bookstore aisles. In the hopes of doing something more manly than shoveling copies of Steinbeck, London, Kerouac and Thoreau onto the floor as they cleared the shelves, the Billys took to elbowing me out of their way.

Delgatto spun and brushed against me until we were nose to nose. "Quit getting under our feet."

"Sure," I said.

"You foul up this job and I'll bury you behind Kennedy Airport where they'll never find you."

"Okay."

"You think I'm kidding?"

"No."

For good measure he shoved me backwards into the counter and got out his buzz saw. Theresa watched me closely, hoping for some action already, her mouth always luscious and glistening. It took Delgatto only a couple of minutes to shear through the sheet rock and crossbeams before he hit some brick. The Billys took off their shirts and got to work with the sledges, keeping the Glocks in their shoulder holsters so they could slick the leather with sweat. They did their best to inject a little swagger in their waddles and keep their stomachs sucked in.

Theresa kept a firm grip on Mozzy, who looked keenly around and took the whole set-up in. Tonight he was going light and only wearing a diamond heart pendant with a floating bezel set going for around three-quarters of million. I told her, "I don't know what you're waiting for."

"Just wanted to watch a smooth operation like this, Joseph. It's important for a young woman to see various elements of the world at work."

"You shouldn't have come."

"Now why would you say that?"

"There's always a chance of trouble."

"Oh really?" she said, smiling, still bored but having at least a little fun now as the friction began to build. "Not with you in charge."

One of the Billys stepped back and brought his sledge around so that the handle caught me in the ribs. Maybe he was clumsy or maybe he was still trying to make an impression, but enough was enough. I could taste the pain rising in my throat like a bittersweet flavor, and the edges of my vision paled as I heard Theresa give a throaty *humm*—the same kind she sometimes made when we were in bed together. But all of that fell away when I spotted Mozzy staring off at a wrought-iron spiral staircase at the back of the room. I checked too, and saw somebody's foot resting lightly on the top step.

Mozzarella jumped free of Theresa's arms and, side by side, he and I walked to the staircase and looked up to see the frightened woman huddled against the rail. She had bobbed brown hair, a smattering of caramel-colored freckles, and thick glasses that somehow made her extremely cute. She wore jeans and a black T-shirt that hugged her perfectly and showed off every curve and intersection.

"Hi," I said.

"Hello." As scared as she was, she followed through. I liked that.

"Would you come down here, please?"

"Okay." She took the spiral staircase easily, without a sound, to stand next to me. I caught a hint of lilac perfume and some fruity shampoo. She was a head taller than me and probably had me by twenty pounds, but it was all solid.

"You live up there?"

"I own this store. If I'm working late I sometimes stay over on a cot upstairs."

"Oh, I see."

Theresa kept watching me, stroking Mozzy and smiling with that wet mouth, her eyebrows arching, the set of her features so self-assured that I could imagine her on the stand in front of the Grand Jury, completely composed and untouchable. A vein in her throat snapped, and even Mozzy started to look uncomfortable.

"Sorry about the wall," I said to the lady. She stared at the books being trampled under the Billys' feet and her bottom lip started to tremble. That didn't surprise me, I sort of got sick seeing them destroy literature as well. I loved reading Steinbeck and Kerouac. She held her hand to her face and her glasses began to mist. Abruptly she fell forward into my arms and sobbed against my chest. I patted her back and tried to keep from saying, "There, there," but was at a loss and couldn't help myself. "There, there."

The Billys kept working at the brick, throwing sparks whenever the sledges hit. Delgatto turned to protect his eyes and saw the woman crying as I consoled her. He showed me all of his teeth. He shouted, "Where the hell did she come from!"

"She owns the store and stays upstairs."

"Oh fer . . . ! Can't I turn my back for ten minutes! Did she call the cops?"

"Did you call the cops?" I asked her.

"No," she said between sobs. "There's no phone up there."

"No," I said to Delgatto. "There's no phone up there."

His upper lip peeled back in a wolf's leer and he made a motion to me with his chin. I shrugged and he did it again, and again, until I finally realized it was sort of a "cut her throat" gesture. He really was a ridiculous bastard. I stared calmly at him until he turned back to the wall and he and the Billys got back to work.

She finished sniffling and looked up at me. "You people are jewel thieves?"

"Uhm, well," I said. "Technically, I'm not. I just came along because of the cat."

Theresa took it in stride, everything just another part of the festivities this evening. "Who are you?" she asked.

"My name is Margaret."

"Hi, I'm Joseph," I told her.

"Pleased to meet you."

Theresa sighed and said, "Margaret, if you try to run, we'll splash your ugly brains all over these stupid books of yours."

Margaret stood there and started crying again.

Theresa gave me the smile, which was even pinker than it had been before. "Nice," I said. "You talk to all the boys at the sophomore mixers like that?"

A crash of crumbling brick resounded in the shop and Delgatto said, "We're in." He and the Billys vanished inside, where they wasted no time shattering glass cases and stuffing their sacks—they really had sacks, no briefcases, no bags, but sacks—full of watches, broaches, necklaces and gemstone earrings. I only saw a few diamond displays. I lifted Mozzarella from Theresa's arms and set him loose in the jewelry shop. "Go get yourself something nice, Mozzy."

He dipped and weaved while I kept an eye on the crew to make sure they weren't taking more than they should be. Mozzy stretched, pranced and hopped up onto one of the display cases and sat expectantly, sort of frowning. Margaret sidled up beside me and said, "You let the cat get the jewels?"

"Only the diamonds."

She thought about it for a second. "You are one seriously messed up wise guy."

"Don't I know it."

I watched as they loaded up about three million in jewelry, and knew that no matter how much they stole they'd still never buy a suit from anywhere but off the rack. Mozzarella sat on top of a case, his tail flicking. I stepped over and slid open the unlocked glass door. I took out the half-carat teardrop diamond necklace within. "Nice rock, Mozzy." Beside it was a pair of earrings, which I also slipped into my pocket.

Delgatto cleaned out the rest of the diamonds, put them in a separate sack and handed them to me. "We're outta here!" he said. I checked my watch. Five minutes since they first stepped inside. Not bad for four guys who collectively had the grace of a crippled water buffalo.

We rounded up and I said, "Margaret, go upstairs. Sorry again about the damage." I gave her the earrings and her eyes lit up, and as she stepped back on the wrought-iron spiral staircase I sighed at the shapeliness of her body.

Delgatto got nice and crimson under his ears. "How do we know she didn't call the cops?"

"I already told you. There's no phone upstairs."

"What're you, nuts? We can't just leave her. She's seen us all. You introduced yourself, fer Chrissake!"

He drew his Glock and that taste flooded my mouth again as I stepped into him, catching his wrist in my right hand and pulling him past me. The Billys moved in slow motion, going for their pieces. I brought my fist hard against Delgatto's elbow, hearing it crack, and pushed him backwards into the middle Billy. The two others lurched forward and I went down to my knees and reached out. Those stupid ankle holsters came in handy as I grabbed the .22s off their legs.

I put a bullet in each of their left kneecaps, and listened to them yowl in tune, hitting the high F. Mozzarella sang with them for a minute and then leaped into Margaret's arms. Theresa squealed in a way that made my breath hitch. Delgatto had his Glock out but couldn't do anything with it. To make sure I put a bullet in his other elbow and then fired at the last Billy's kneecap as well. They rolled and called on the Virgin Mary and begged for their priests. Theresa came up behind me and started biting my ear, the way she did when we were really cooking.

"Now her, Joseph," she said.

"In case you missed it, I just shot these four idiots to save her," I said.

"You know you can't let her walk out of here. You know she can finger us."

"Theresa, please, come on, let's just go, huh?"

"Finish it or you'll be finished. When my grandfather dies I'm taking over the Family. It's going to be like the old days, Joseph. We're going to expand and turn up the heat, and I'm not about to start off with a witness. Finish it, damn it."

The Capeesh might have forgotten who I was by now, and Nicky Francesi would cut me a lot of slack considering all we'd been through together, but Theresa Capesci would never give in. She'd crush anyone who went up against her, hunt them down into the dust for any reason. She'd never let me go.

"I told you that you shouldn't have come," I said, and shot her right in that delicious smile.

It wasn't until I was nearly to Broadway that I realized Margaret was walking next to me, still holding the cat. Mozzarella's ice glittered under the street lamps.

"How's the store doing?" I asked.

"They just opened another Barnes and Noble three blocks away and I've already lost twenty percent of my sales. Anyway, I don't have the kind of insurance that'll cover what you people did in there tonight. I guess I'll have to move." After another three blocks she said, "Thanks for the earrings. You're really nice."

She could stand to lose fifteen pounds but she had something I really liked. I figured she could make a hell of a pot of *pasta fagoli* too.

"You ever been bowling in Idaho?" I asked.

The Maggody Files: Hillbilly Cat

Joan Hess

I was reduced to whittling away the morning, and trying to convince myself that I was in some obscure way whittling away at the length of my sentence in Maggody, Arkansas (pop. 755). Outside the red-bricked PD, the early morning rain came down steadily, and, as Ruby Bee Hanks (proprietress of a bar and grill of the same name, and, incidentally, my mother) would say, it was turning a mite crumpy. I figured the local criminal elements would be daunted enough to stay home, presuming they were smart enough to come in out of the rain in the first place. This isn't to say they rampaged when the sun shone. Mostly they ran the stoplight, fussed and cussed at their neighbors, stole such precious commodities as superior huntin' dawgs, and occasionally raced away from the self-service station without paying for gas. There'd been some isolated violence during my tenure, but every last person in town still based their historical perspective on before-or-after Hiram Buchanon's barn burned to the ground.

I suppose I ought to mention that my sentence was self-imposed, in that I scampered home from Manhattan to lick my wounds after a nasty divorce. In that I was the only person stupid enough to apply for the job, I was not only the Chief of Police, but also the entirety of the department. For a while I'd had a deputy, who just happened to be the mayor's cousin,

149

but he'd gotten himself in trouble over his unrequited love for a bosomy barmaid. Now I had a beeper.

That October morning I had a block of balsa wood that was harder than granite, and a pocket knife that was duller than most of the population. I also had some bizarre dreams of converting the wood into something that remotely resembled a duck—a marshland mallard, to be precise. Those loyal souls who're schooled in the local lore know I tried this a while back, with zero success. Same wood, for the record, and thus far, same rate of success.

So I had my feet on the corner of my desk, my cane-bottomed chair propped back against the wall, and an unholy mess of wood shavings scattered all over the place when the door opened. The man who came in wore a black plastic raincoat and was wrestling with a brightly striped umbrella more suited to a swanky golf course (in Maggody, we don't approve of golf—or any other sissified sport in which grown men wear shorts). He appeared to be forty or so, with a good ol' boy belly and the short, wavy hair of a used car salesman.

Strangers come into the PD maybe three times a year, usually to ask directions or to sell me subscriptions to magazines like *Field and Stream* or *Sports Illustrated*. I guess it's never occurred to any of them that some of us backwoods cops might prefer *Cosmopolitan*.

He finally gave up on the umbrella and set it in a corner to drip. Flashing two rows of pearly white teeth at me, he said, "Hey, honey, some weather, isn't it? Is the chief in?"

"It sure is some weather," I said politely, "and the chief is definitely in." I did not add that the chief was mildly insulted, but by no means incensed or inclined to explain further.

This time I got a wink. "Could I have a word with him?"

"You're having a word with *her* at this very moment," I said as I dropped my duck in a drawer and crossed my arms, idly wondering how long it'd take him to work it out. He didn't look downright stupid like the clannish Buchanons, who're obliged to operate solely on animal instinct, but he had squinty eyes, flaccid lips, and minutes earlier had lost a battle to an umbrella.

"Sorry, honey." His shrug indicated he wasn't altogether overwhelmed with remorse. "I'm Nelson Mullein from down near Pine Bluff. The woman at the hardware store said the chief's name was Arly, and I sort of assumed I was looking for a fellow. My mistake."

"How may I help you, Mr. Mullein?" I said.

"Call me Nelson, please. My great-grandaunts live here in Maggody, out on County 102 on the other side of the low water bridge. Everybody's always called them the Banebury girls, although Miss Columbine is seventy-eight and Miss Larkspur's seventy-six."

"I know who they are."

"Thought you might." He sat down on the chair across from my desk and took out a cigar. When he caught my glare, he replaced it in his pocket, licked his lips, and made a production of grimacing and sighing so I'd appreciate how carefully he was choosing his words. "The thing is," he said slowly, "I'm worried about them. As I said, they're old and they live in that big, ramshackle house by themselves. It ain't in the ghetto, but it's a far cry from suburbia. Neither one of them can see worth a damn. Miss Larkspur took a fall last year while she was climbing out of the tub; and her hip healed so poorly she's still using a walker. Miss Columbine is wheezier than a leaky balloon."

"So I should arrest them for being old and frail?"

"Of course not," he said, massaging his rubbery jowls. "I was hoping you could talk some sense into them, that's all, 'cause I sure as hell can't, even though I'm their only relative.

151

It hurts me to see them living the way they do. They're as poor as church mice. When I went out there yesterday, it was colder inside than it was outside, and the only heat was from a wood fire in a potbelly stove. Seems they couldn't pay the gas bill last month and it was shut off. I took care of that immediately and told the Gas Company to bill me in the future. If Miss Columbine finds out, she'll have a fit, but I didn't know what else to do."

He sounded so genuinely concerned that I forgave him for calling me "honey," and tried to recall what little I knew about the Banebury girls. They'd been reclusive even when I was a kid, although they occasionally drove through town in a glossy black Lincoln Continental, nodding regally at the peasants. One summer night twenty or so years ago, they'd caught a gang of us skinny-dipping at the far side of the field behind their house. Miss Columbine had been outraged. After she'd carried on for a good ten minutes, Miss Larkspur persuaded her not to report the incident to our parents and we grabbed our clothes and hightailed it. We stayed well downstream the rest of the summer. We avoided their house at Halloween, but only because it was isolated and not worth the risk of having to listen to a lecture on hooliganism in exchange for a stale popcorn ball.

"I understand your concern," I said. "I'm afraid I don't know them well enough to have any influence."

"They told me they still drive. Miss Columbine has macular degeneration, which means her peripheral vision's fine but she can't see anything in front of her. Miss Larkspur's legally blind, but that works out just fine—she navigates. I asked them how on earth either had a driver's license, and damned if they didn't show 'em to me. The date was 1974."

I winced. "Maybe once or twice a year, they drive half a

mile to church at a speed of no more than ten miles an hour. When they come down the middle of the road, everybody in town knows to pull over, all the way into a ditch if need be, and the children have been taught to do their rubberneckin' from their yards. It's actually kind of a glitzy local event that's discussed for days afterwards. I realize it's illegal, but I'm not about to go out there and tell them they can't drive anymore."

"Yeah, I know," he said, "but I'm going to lose a lot of sleep if I don't do something for them. I'm staying at a motel in Farberville. This morning I got on the phone and found out about a retirement facility for the elderly. I went out and looked at it, and it's more like a boardinghouse than one of those smelly nursing homes. Everybody has a private bedroom, and meals are provided in a nice, warm dining room. There was a domino game going on while I was there, and a couple of the women were watching a soap opera. There's a van to take them shopping or to doctor appointments. It's kind of expensive, but I think I can swing it by using their social security checks and setting up an income from the sale of the house and property. I had a real estate agent drive by it this morning, and he thought he could get eight, maybe ten, thousand dollars."

"And when you presented this, they said . . . ?"

"Miss Columbine's a hardheaded woman, and she liked to scorch my ears," he admitted ruefully. "I felt like I was ten years old and been caught with a toad in the pocket of my choir robe. Miss Larkspur was interested at first, and asked some questions, but when they found out they couldn't take Eppie, the discussion was over, and before I knew what hit me, I was out on the porch shivering like a hound dog in a blizzard."

"Eppie?"

"Their cat. In spite of the sweet-sounding name, it's an obese yellow tomcat with one eye and a tattered ear. It's mangy and mean and moth-eaten, and that's being charitable. But they won't even consider giving it away, and the residence home forbids pets because of a health department regulation. I went ahead and put down a deposit, but the director said she can't hold the rooms for more than a few days and she expects to be filled real soon. I hate to say it, but it's now or never." He spread his hands and gave me a beseeching look. "Do you think you or anybody else in town can talk them into at least taking a look at this place?"

I suspected I would have more luck with my balsa wood than with the Banebury sisters, but I promised Nelson I'd give it a shot and wrote down the telephone number of his motel room. After a display of effusively moist gratitude, he left.

I decided the matter could wait until after lunch. The Banebury sisters had been going about their business nearly four score years, after all, I told myself righteously as I darted through the drizzle to my car and headed for Ruby Bee's Bar & Grill.

"So what's this about Miss Columbine and Miss Larkspur being dragged off to an old folks' home?" Ruby Bee demanded as I walked across the tiny dance floor. It was too early for the noon crowd, and only one booth was occupied by a pair of truck drivers working on blue-plate specials and a pitcher of beer.

"And who'd pay ten thousand dollars for that old shack?" Estelle Oppers added from her favorite stool at the end of the bar, convenient to the pretzels and the rest room.

I wasn't particularly amazed by the questions. Maggody has a very sturdy grapevine, and it definitely curls through the barroom on its way from one end of town to the other. That was one of the reasons I'd left the day after I graduated, and eventually took refuge in the anonymity of Manhattan, where one can caper in the nude on the street and no one so much as bothers with a second look. In Maggody, you can hear about what you did before you're finished planning to do it.

"To think they'd give up their cat!" Ruby Bee continued, her hands on her hips and her eyes flashing as if I'd suggested we drown dear Eppie in Boone Creek. Beneath her unnaturally blond hair, her face was screwed up with indignation. "It ain't much to look at, but they've had it for fourteen years and some folks just don't understand how attached they are."

I opened my mouth to offer a mild rebuttal, but Estelle leapt in with the agility of a trout going after a mayfly. "Furthermore, I think it's mighty suspicious, him coming to town all of a sudden to disrupt their lives. I always say, when there's old ladies and a cat, the nephew's up to no good. Just last week I read a story about how the nephew tried to trick his aunt so he could steal all her money."

I chose a stool at the opposite end of the bar. "From what Nelson told me, they don't have any money."

"I still say he's up to no good," Estelle said mulishly, which is pretty much the way she said everything.

Ruby Bee took a dishrag and began to wipe the pristine surface of the bar. "I reckon that much is true, but Eula said she happened to see him in the hardware store, and he had a real oily look about him, like a carnival roustabout. She said she wouldn't have been surprised if he had tattoos under his clothes. He was asking all kinds of questions, too."

"Like what?" I said, peering at the pies under glass domes and ascertaining there was a good-sized piece of cherry left.

"Well, he wanted to know where to go to have all their utility bills sent to him, on account of he didn't think they had

155

enough money to pay 'em. He also wanted to know if he could arrange for groceries to be delivered to their house every week, but Eula stepped in and explained that the church auxiliary already sees to that."

I shook my head and made a clucking noise. "The man's clearly a scoundrel, a cad, a veritable devil in disguise. How about meatloaf, mashed potatoes and gravy, and cherry pie with ice cream?"

Ruby Bee was not in her maternal mode. "And wasn't there an old movie about a smarmy nephew trying to put his sweet old aunts in some sort of insane asylum?" she asked Estelle.

"That was because they were poisoning folks. I don't recollect anyone accusing the Banebury girls of anything like that. Miss Columbine's got a sharp tongue, but she's got her wits about her. I wish I could say the same thing about Miss Larkspur. She can be kind of silly and forgetful, but she ain't got a mean bone in her body. Now if the cat was stalking me on a dark street, I'd be looking over my shoulder and fearing for my life. He lost his eye in a fight with old Shep Humes's pit bull. When Shep tried to pull 'em apart, he liked to lose both of his eyes and a couple of fingers, and he said he cain't remember when he heard a gawdawful racket like that night."

"Meatloaf?" I said optimistically. "Mashed potatoes?"

Still wiping the bar, Ruby Bee worked her way towards Estelle. "The real estate agent says he can sell that place for ten thousand dollars?"

"He didn't sound real sure of it, and Eilene said Earl said the fellow didn't think the house was worth a dollar. It was the forty acres he thought might sell." Estelle popped a pretzel in her mouth and chewed it pensively. "I took them a basket of cookies last year just before Christmas, and the house is in such sad shape that I thought to myself, I'm gonna sit right down and cry. The plaster's crumbling off the walls, and there was more than one window taped with cardboard. It's a matter of time before the house falls down on 'em."

Aware I was about to go down for the third time, I said, "Meatloaf?"

Ruby Bee leaned across the bar, and in a melodramatic whisper that most likely was audible in the next county, said, "Do you think they're misers with a fortune buried in jars in the back yard? If this Mullein fellow knows it, then he'd want to get rid of them and have all the time he needs to dig up the yard searching for the money."

"Them?" Estelle cackled. "There was some family money when their daddy owned the feed store, but he lost so much money when that fancy co-op opened in Starley City that he lost the store and upped and died within the year. After that, Miss Larkspur had to take piano students and Miss Columbine did mending until they went on social security. Now how are they supposed to have acquired this fortune? Are you accusing them of putting on ski masks and robbing liquor stores?"

"For pity's sake, I was just thinking out loud," Ruby Bee retorted.

"The next thing, you'll be saying you saw them on that television show about unsolved crimes."

"At least some of us have better things to do than read silly mystery stories about nephews and cats," Ruby Bee said disdainfully. "I wouldn't be surprised if you didn't have a whole book filled with them."

"So what if I do?" Estelle slapped the bar hard enough to tump the pretzels.

It seemed the only thing being served was food for thought. I drove to the Dairee Dee-Lishus and ate a chilidog in my car while I fiddled with the radio in search of anything but whiny country music. I was doing so to avoid thinking about the conversation at Ruby Bee's. Nelson Mullein wasn't my type, but that didn't automatically relegate him to the slime pool. He had good reason to be worried about his great-grandaunts. Hell, now I was worried about them, too.

Then again, I thought as I drove out County 102 and eased across the low-water bridge, Estelle had a point. There was something almost eerie about the combination of old ladies, cats, and ne'er-do-well nephews (although, as far as I knew, Nelson was doing well at whatever he did; I hadn't asked). But we were missing the key element in the plot, and that was the fortune that kicked in the greed factor. Based on what Estelle had said, the Banebury girls were just as poor as Nelson had claimed.

The appearance of the house confirmed it. It was a squatty old farmhouse that had once been white, but was weathered to a lifeless gray. What shingles remained on the roof were mossy, and the chimney had collapsed. A window on the second floor was covered with cardboard; broken glass was scattered on the porch. The detached garage across the weedy yard had fared no better.

Avoiding puddles, I hurried to the front door and knocked, keenly and uncomfortably aware of the icy rain slithering under my collar. I was about to knock a second time when the door opened a few cautious inches.

"I'm Arly Hanks," I said, trying not to let my teeth chatter too loudly. "Do you mind if I come in for a little visit?"

"I reckon you can." Miss Columbine stepped back and gestured for me to enter. To my astonishment, she looked almost exactly the same as she had the night she stood on the bank of Boone Creek and bawled us out. Her hair was white and pinned up in tight braids, her nose was sharp, her cheekbones prominent above concave cheeks. Her head was tilted at an angle, and I remembered what Nelson had said about her vision.

"Thanks," I murmured as I rubbed my hands together.

"Hanks, did you say? You're Ruby Bee's gal," she said in the same steely voice. "Now that you're growed up, are you keeping your clothes on when you take a moonlight swim?"

I was reduced to an adolescent, "Yes, ma'am."

"Do we have a visitor?" Miss Larkspur came into the living room, utilizing an aluminum walker to take each awkward step. "First Nelson and now this girl. I swear, I don't know when we've had so much company, Columbine."

The twenty years had been less compassionate to Miss Larkspur. Her eyes were so clouded and her skin so translucent that she looked as if she'd been embalmed. Her body was bent, one shoulder hunched and the other undefined. The fingers that gripped the walker were swollen and misshapen.

"I'm Arly Hanks," I told her.

"Gracious, girl, I know who you are. I heard about how you came back to Maggody after all those years in the big city. I don't blame you one bit. Columbine and I went to visit kin in Memphis when we were youngsters, and I knew then and there that I'd never be able to live in a place like that. There were so many cars and carriages and streetcars that we feared for our very lives, didn't we?"

"Yes, I seem to recall that we did, Larkspur."

"Shall I put on the tea kettle?"

Miss Columbine smiled sadly. "That's all right, sister; I'll see to it. Why don't you sit down with our company while I fix a tray? Be sure and introduce her to Eppie."

The room was scantily furnished with ugly, battered furniture and a rug worn so badly that the wooden floor was visible. It smelled of decay, and no doubt for a very good reason. Plaster had fallen in several places, exposing the joists and yellowed newspaper that served as insulation. Although it was warmer than outside, it was a good twenty degrees below what I considered comfortable. Both sisters wore shawls. I hoped they had thermal underwear beneath their plain, dark dresses.

I waited until Miss Larkspur had made it across the room and was seated on a sofa. I sat across from her and said, "I met Nelson this morning. He seems concerned about you and your sister."

"So he says," she said without interest. She leaned forward and clapped her hands. "Eppie? Are you hiding? It's quite safe to come out. This girl won't hurt you. She'd like the chance to admire you."

An enormous cat stalked from behind the sofa, his single amber eye regarding me malevolently and his tail swishing as if he considered it a weapon. He was everything Nelson had described, and worse. He paused to rake his claws across the carpet, then leapt into Miss Larkspur's lap and settled down to convey to me how very deeply he resented my presence. Had I been a less rational person, I would have wondered if he knew I was there to promote Nelson's plan. Had I been, as I said.

"Isn't he a pretty kitty?" cooed Miss Larkspur. "He acts so big and tough, but him's just a snuggly teddy bear."

"Very pretty," I said, resisting an urge to lapse into baby talk and tweak Eppie's whiskers. He would have taken my hand off in a flash. Or my arm.

Miss Columbine came into the room, carrying a tray with three cups and saucers and a ceramic teapot. There were more chips than rosebuds, but I was delighted to take a cup of hot tea and cradle it in my hands. "Did Nelson send you?" she said as she served her sister and sat down beside her. Eppie snuggled between them to continue his surly surveillance.

"He came by the PD this morning and asked me to speak to you," I admitted.

"Nelson is a ninny," she said with a tight frown. "Always has been, always will be. When he came during the summers, I had to watch him like a hawk to make sure he wasn't tormenting the cat or stealing pennies from the sugar bowl. His grandmother, our youngest sister, married poor white trash, and although she never said a word against them, we were all of a mind that she regretted it to her dying day." She paused to take a sip of tea, and the cup rattled against the saucer as she replaced it. "I suppose Nelson's riled up on account of our Sunday drives, although it seems to me reporting us to the police is extreme. Did you come out here to arrest us?"

Miss Larkspur giggled. "What would Papa say if he were here to see us being arrested? Can't you imagine the look on his face, Columbine? He'd be fit to be tied, and he'd most likely throw this nice young thing right out the door."

"I didn't come out here to arrest you," I said hastily, "and I didn't come to talk about your driving. As long as you don't run anybody down, stay on this road, and never ever go on the highway, it's okay with me."

"But not with Nelson." Miss Columbine sighed as she finished her tea. "He wants us to give up our home, our car, our beloved Eppie, and go live in a stranger's house with a bunch of old folks. Who knows what other fool rules they'd have in a house where they don't allow pets?"

"But, Columbine," Miss Larkspur said, her face puckering wistfully, "Nelson says they serve nice meals and have tea with sandwiches and pound cake every afternoon. I can't recollect when I last tasted pound cake—unless it was at Mama's last birthday party. She died of influenza back in September of fifty-eight, not three weeks after Papa brought the new car all the way from Memphis, Tennessee." She took a tissue from her cuff and dabbed her eyes. "Papa died the next year, some say on account of losing the store, but I always thought he was heartsick over poor—"

"Larkspur, you're rambling like a wild turkey," Columbine said sternly but with affection. "This girl doesn't want to hear our family history. Frankly, I don't find it that interesting. I think we'd better hear what she has to say so she can be on her way." She stroked Eppie's head, and the cat obligingly growled at yours truly.

"Is Eppie the only reason you won't consider this retirement house?" I asked. I realized it was not such an easy question and plunged ahead. "You don't have to make a decision until you've visited. I'm sure Nelson would be delighted to take you there at tea time."

"Do you think he would?" Miss Larkspur clasped her hands together and her cloudy eyes sparkled briefly.

Miss Columbine shook her head. "We cannot visit under false pretenses, Larkspur, and come what may, we will not abandon Eppie after all these years. When the Good Lord sees fit to take him from us, we'll think about moving to town."

The object of discussion stretched his front legs and squirmed until he was on his back, his claws digging into their legs demandingly. When Miss Columbine rubbed his bloated belly, he purred with all the delicacy of a truck changing gears.

"Thank you for tea," I said, rising. "I'll let myself out." I was almost at the front door when I stopped and turned back to them. "You won't be driving until Easter, will you?"

"Not until Easter," Miss Columbine said firmly.

I returned to the PD, dried myself off with a handful of paper towels, and called Nelson at the motel to report my failure.

"It's the cat, isn't it?" he said. "They're willing to live in squalor because they won't give up that sorry excuse for a cat. You know, honey, I'm beginning to wonder if they haven't wandered too far out in left field to know what's good for them. I guess I'd better talk to a lawyer when I get back to Pine Bluff."

"You're going to force them to move?"

"I feel so bad, honey, but I don't know what else to do and it's for their own good."

"What's in it for you, Nelson?"

"Nothing." He banged down the receiver.

"My shoe's full of water," Ruby Bee grumbled as she did her best to avoid getting smacked in the face by a bunch of soggy leaves. It wasn't all that easy, since she had to keep her flashlight trained on the ground in case of snakes or other critters. The worst of it was that Estelle had hustled her out the door on this harebrained mission without giving her a chance to change clothes, and now her best blue dress was splattered with mud and her matching blue suede shoes might as well go straight into the garbage can. "Doncha think it's time to stop acting like overgrown Girl Scouts and just drive up to the door, knock real politely, and ask our questions in the living room?"

Estelle was in the lead, mostly because she had the better flashlight. "At least it's stopped raining, Miss Moanie Mouth. You're carrying on like we had to go miles and miles, but it ain't more than two hundred feet to begin with and we're within spittin' distance already."

"I'd be within spittin' distance of my bed if we'd dropped in and asked them." Ruby Bee stepped over a log and right into a puddle, this time filling her other shoe with cold water and forcing her to bite her tongue to keep from blurting out something unseemly. However, she figured she'd better pay more attention to the job at hand, which was sneaking up on the Banebury girls' garage through the woods behind it.

"I told you so," Estelle said as she flashed her light on the backside of the building. "Now turn out your light and stay real close. If that door's not locked, we'll be inside quicker than a preacher says his prayers at night."

The proverbial preacher would have had time to bless a lot of folks. The door wasn't locked, but it was warped something awful and it took a good five minutes of puffing and grunting to get it open far enough for them to slip inside.

Ruby Bee stopped to catch her breath. "I still don't see why you're so dadburned worried about them seeing us. They're both blind as bats."

"Hush!" Estelle played her light over the black sedan. "Lordy, they made 'em big in those days, didn't they? You could put one of those little Japanese cars in the trunk of this one, and have enough room left for a table and four chairs. And look at all that chrome!"

"This ain't the showroom of a car dealership," Ruby Bee said in the snippety voice that always irritated Estelle, which was exactly what she intended for it to do, what with her ruined shoes and toes nigh onto frozen. "If you want to stand there and admire it all night, that's fine, but I for one have other plans. I'll see if it says the model on the back, and you try the interior."

She was shining her light on the license plate and calculating how many years it had been since it expired when Estelle screamed. Before she could say a word, Estelle dashed out the door, the beam from the flashlight bobbling like a ping-pong ball. Mystified but not willing to linger on her own, Ruby Bee followed as fast as she dared, and only when she caught Estelle halfway through the woods did she learn what had caused the undignified retreat.

According to Estelle, there'd been a giant rat right in the front seat of the car, its lone amber eye glaring like the devil's own. Ruby Bee snorted in disbelief, but she didn't go back to have a look for herself.

The next morning, sweet inspiration slapped me up the side of the head like a two by four. It had to be the car. I lunged for the telephone so hastily that my poor duck fell to the floor, and called Plover, a state cop with whom I occasionally went to a movie or had dinner. "What do you know about antique cars?" I demanded, bypassing pleasantries.

"They're old. Some of them are real old."

"Did you forget to jump start your brain this morning? I need to find out the current value of a particular car, and I assumed you were up on something macho like this."

He let out a long-suffering sort of sigh. "I can put gas in one at the self-service pump, and I know how to drive it. That's the extent of my so-called macho knowledge."

"Jesus, Plover," I said with a sigh of my own, "you'd better get yourself a frilly pink skirt and a pair of high heel sneakers. While you're doing that, let me talk to someone in the barracks with balls who knows about cars, okay?"

He hung up on what I thought was a very witty remark. State cops were not renowned for their humor, I told myself as I flipped open the telephone directory and hunted up the number of the Lincoln dealer in Farberville. The man who answered was a helluva lot more congenial, possibly (and mistakenly) in hopes he was dealing with a potential buyer.

Alas, he was no better informed than Plover about the current market value of a '58 Lincoln Continental, but his attitude was much brighter and he promised to call me back as soon as possible.

Rather than waste the time patting myself on the back, I called Plover, apologized for my smart-mouthed remark, and explained what I surmised was going on. "It's the car he's after," I concluded. "The house and land are close to worthless, but this old Lincoln could be a collector's dream."

"Maybe," he said without conviction, "but you can't arrest him for anything. I don't know if what he tried to do constitutes fraud, but in any case, he failed. He can't get his hands on the car until they die."

"Or he has them declared incompetent," I said. "I suppose I could let him know that I'm aware of his scheme, and that I'll testify on their behalf if he tries anything further."

We chatted aimlessly for a while, agreed to a dinner date in a few days, and hung up. I was preparing to dial the number of Nelson's motel room when the phone rang.

The dealer had my information. I grabbed a pencil and wrote down a few numbers, thanked him, and replaced the receiver with a scowl of disappointment. If the car was in mint condition (aka in its original wrapper), it might bring close to ten thousand dollars. The amounts then plummeted: sixty-five hundred for very good, less than five thousand for good, and on down to four hundred fifty as a source for parts.

It wasn't the car, after all, but simply a case of letting myself listen to the suspicious minds in Ruby Bee's Bar & Grill. I picked up the balsa wood and turned my attention to its little webbed feet.

It normally doesn't get dark until five-thirty or so, but the heavy clouds had snuffed out the sunset. I decided to call it a day (not much of one, though) and find out if Ruby Bee was in a more hospitable mood. I had locked the back door and switched off the light when the telephone rang. After a short debate centering around meatloaf versus professional obligations, I reluctantly picked up the receiver.

"Arly! You got to do something! Somebody's gonna get killed if you don't do something!"

"Calm down, Estelle," I said, regretting that I hadn't heeded the plea from my stomach. "What's the problem?"

"I'm so dadburned all shook up I can barely talk!"

I'd had too much experience with her to be overcome with alarm. "Give it your best shot."

"It's the Banebury girls! They just drove by my house, moving real smartly down the middle of the road, and no headlights! I was close enough to my driveway to whip in and get out of their way, but I'm thanking my lucky stars I saw 'em before they ran me over with that bulldozer of a car."

I dropped the receiver, grabbed my car keys, and ran out to the side of the highway. I saw nothing coming from the south, but if they were driving without lights, I wouldn't be the only one not to see them coming . . . relentlessly, in a great black death machine.

"Damn!" I muttered as I got in my car, maneuvered around, and headed down the highway to the turnoff for County 102. Miss Columbine couldn't see anything in front of her, and Miss Larkspur was legally blind. A dynamite duo. I muttered a lot more things, none of them acceptable within my mother's earshot.

It was supper time, and the highway was blessedly empty. I squealed around the corner and stopped, letting my lights shine down the narrow road. The wet pavement glistened like a snakeskin. They had passed Estelle's house at least three or four minutes ago. Presuming they were not in a ditch, they would arrive at the intersection any minute. Maybe Nelson had a justifiable reason to have them declared incompetent, I thought as I gripped the steering wheel and peered into the darkness. I hadn't seen any bunnies hopping outside my window, and if there were chocolate eggs hidden in the PD, I hadn't found them.

It occurred to me that I was in more than minimal danger, parked as I was in their path. However, I couldn't let them go on their merry way. A conscientious cop would have forbidden them to drive and confiscated the keys. I'd practically given them my blessing.

My headlights caught the glint of a massive black hood bearing down on me. With a yelp, I changed the beam to high, fumbled with a switch until the blue light on the roof began to rotate, grabbed a flashlight, and jumped out of my car. I waved the light back and forth as the monster bore down on me, and I had some sharp insights into the last thoughts of potential roadkill.

All I could see was the reflection on the chrome as the car came at me, slowly yet determinedly. The blue light splashed on the windshield, as did my flashlight. "Miss Columbine!" I yelled. "Miss Larkspur! You've got to stop!" I retreated behind my car and continued yelling.

The car shuddered, then, at the last moment, stopped a good six inches from my bumper (and a six-hour session with the mayor, trying to explain the bill from the body shop).

I pried my teeth off my lower lip, switched off the flashlight, and went to the driver's window. Miss Columbine sat rigidly behind the wheel, but Miss Larkspur leaned forward and, with a little wave, said, "It's Arly, isn't it? How are you, dear?"

"Much better than I was a minute ago," I said. "I thought we agreed that you wouldn't be driving until this spring, Miss Columbine. A day later you're not only out, but at night without headlights."

"When you're blind," she said tartly, "darkness is not a factor. This is an emergency. Since we don't have a telephone, we had no choice but to drive for help."

"That's right," said Miss Larkspur. "Eppie has been cat-napped. We're beside ourselves with worry. He likes to roam around the yard during the afternoon, but this evening he did not come to the back door to demand his supper. Columbine and I searched as best we could, but poor Eppie has disappeared. It's not like him, not at all."

"Larkspur is correct," Miss Columbine added. Despite her gruff voice and expressionless face, a tear trickled down her cheek. She wiped it away and tilted her head to look at me. "I am loath to go jumping to conclusions, but in this case, it's hard not to."

"I agree," I said, gazing bleakly at the darkness surrounding us. It may not have been a factor for them, but it sure as hell was for me. "Let's go back to your place and I'll try to find Eppie. Maybe he's already on the porch, waiting to be fed. I'll move my car off the road, and then, if you don't object, I think it's safer for me to drive your car back for you."

A few minutes later I was sitting in the cracked leather upholstery of the driver's seat, trying to figure out the controls on the elaborate wooden dashboard. There was ample room for three of us in the front seat, and possibly a hitchhiker or two. Once I'd found first gear, I turned around in the church parking lot, took a deep breath, and let 'er fly.

"This is a daunting machine," I said.

Giggling, Miss Larkspur put her hand on my arm and said, "Papa brought it all the way from Memphis, as I told you. He'd gone there on account of Cousin Pearl being at the hospital, and we were flabbergasted when he drove up a week later in a shiny new car. This was after he'd lost the store, you see, and we didn't even own a car. We felt real badly about him going all the way to Memphis on the bus, but he and Cousin Pearl were kissin' cousins, and she was dying in the Baptist Hospital, so—"

"The Methodist Hospital," Miss Columbine corrected her. "I swear, some days you go on and on like you ain't got a brain in your head. Papa must have told us a hundred times how he met that polite young soldier whose mother was dying in the room right next to Cousin Pearl's."

"I suppose so," Miss Larkspur conceded, "but Cousin Pearl was a Baptist."

I pulled into the rutted driveway beside their house. The garage door was open, so I eased the car inside, turned off the ignition, and leaned back to offer a small prayer. "Why don't you wait in the house? I'll have a look out back."

"I can't believe our own kin would do such a thing," Miss Columbine said as she took Miss Larkspur's arm. I took the other and we moved slowly toward the back porch.

I believed it, and I had a pretty good idea why he'd done it. Once they were inside, I went back to the car, looked at the contents of the glove compartment to confirm my suspicions, and set off across the field. I'd had enough sense to bring my flashlight, but it was still treacherously wet and rough and I wasn't in the mood to end up with my feet in the air and my fanny in the mud: I could think of a much better candidate.

I froze as my light caught a glittery orb moving toward me in an erratic pattern. It came closer, and at last I made out Eppie's silhouette as he bounded past me in the direction of the house. His yowl of rage shattered the silence for a heart-stopping moment, then he was gone and I was once again alone in the field with a twenty-year-old memory of the path that led to Boone Creek.

Long before I arrived at the bank, I heard a stream of curses and expletives way too colorful for my sensitive ears. I followed the sound and stopped at a prudent distance to shine my light on Nelson Mullein. He was not a pretty picture as he futilely attempted to slither up the muddy incline, snatching at clumps of weeds that uprooted in his hands. He was soaked to the skin. His face was distorted not only by a swath of mud across one cheek, but also by angry red scratches, some of which were oozing blood.

"Who is it?" he said, blinking into the light.

"It's traditional to take your clothes off when you skinny-dip in the creek."

"It's you, the lady cop." He snatched at a branch, but it broke and he slid back to the edge of the inky water. "Can you give me a hand, honey? It's like trying to climb an oil slick, and I'm about to freeze to death."

"Oh, my goodness," I said as I scanned the ground with the light until it rested on a shapeless brown mound nearby. "Could that be a gunny sack? Why, I do believe it is. I hope you didn't put Eppie in it in an unsuccessful attempt to drown him in the creek."

"I've never seen that before in my life. I came down here to search for the cat. The damn thing was up in that tree, meowing in a right pitiful fashion, but when I tried to coax him down, I lost my footing and fell into the water. Why don't you try to find a sturdy branch so I can get up the bank?"

I squatted next to the gunnysack. "This ol' thing's nearly ripped to shreds. I guess Eppie didn't take kindly to the idea of being sent to Cat Heaven before his time. By the way, I know about the car, Mr. Mullein."

"That jalopy?" he said uneasily. He stopped skittering in the mud and wiped his face. "I reckoned on getting six, maybe seven thousand for it from an ol' boy what lives in Pine Bluff. That, along with the proceeds from the sale of the property, ought to be more than enough to keep my great-grandaunts from living the way they do, bless their brave souls."

"It ought to be more than enough for them to have the house remodeled and pay for a full-time housekeeper," I said as I rose, the gunnysack dangling between my thumb and forefinger. "I'm taking this along as evidence. If you ever again so much as set one foot in Maggody, I'll tell those brave souls what you tried to do. You may be their only relative, but someone might suggest they leave what's going to be in the range of half a million dollars to a rest home for cats!"

"You can't abandon me like this." He gave me a view of his pearly white teeth, but it was more of a snarl than a smile. "Don't be cruel like that, honey."

"Watch me." Ignoring his sputters, I took my tattered treasure and walked back across the field to the house. Miss Columbine took me into the living room, where her sister had swaddled Eppie in a towel.

"Him was just being a naughty kitty," she said, stroking the cat's remaining ear and nuzzling his head.

I accepted a cup of tea, and once we were settled as before, said, "That polite young soldier gave your papa the car, didn't he?"

Miss Columbine nodded. "Papa didn't know what to think, but the boy was insistent about how he'd gone from rags to riches and how it made him feel good to be able to give folks presents. Papa finally agreed, saying it was only on account of how excited Mama would be."

"It was charity, of course," Miss Larkspur added, "but the boy said he wanted to do it because of Papa's kindness in the waiting room. The boy even told Papa that he was a hillbilly cat himself, and never forgot the little town in Mississippi where he was born."

Eppie growled ominously, but I avoided meeting his hostile eye and said, "He was called the Hillbilly Cat, back in the earliest stage of his career. The original paperwork's in the

The Maggody Files: Hillbilly Cat

glove compartment, and his signature is on the bill of sale and registration form." I explained how much the car would bring and agreed to supervise the sale for them. "This means, of course, that you won't be driving anymore," I added.

"But how will we get to church on Easter morning?" Miss Larkspur asked.

Miss Columbine smiled. "I reckon we can afford a limousine, Larkspur. Let's heat up some nice warm milk for Eppie. He's still shivering from his . . . adventure outside."

"Now that we'll be together, will you promise to never run away again?" Miss Larkspur gently scolded the cat.

He looked at her, then at me on the off chance I'd try to pet him and he could express his animosity with his claws.

I waved at him from the doorway, told the ladies I'd be in touch after I talked with the Lincoln dealer, and wished them a pleasant evening. I walked down the road to my car, and I was nearly there before I realized Eppie was a nickname. Once he'd been the Hillbilly Cat, and his death had broken hearts all around the world. But in the Banebury household, Elvis Presley was alive and well—and still the King.

"Give me that shovel," Estelle hissed. "All you're doing is poking the dirt like you think this is a mine field."

Ruby Bee eased the blade into the muddy soil, mindful of the splatters on the hem of her coat and the caked mud that made her shoes feel like combat boots. "Hold your horses," she hissed back, "I heard a clink. I don't want to break the jar and ruin the money."

Estelle hurried over and knelt down to dig with her fingers. "Ain't the Banebury girls gonna be excited when we find their Papa's buried treasure! I reckon we could find as much as a thousand dollars before the night is out." She daintily blotted her forehead with her wrist. "It's a darn shame about the car, but if it ain't worth much, then it ain't. It's kinda funny how that man at the Lincoln dealership rattled off the prices like he had 'em written out in front of him and was wishing somebody'd call to inquire. Of course I wasn't expecting to hear anything different. Everybody knows just because a car's old doesn't mean it's valuable."

A lot of responses went through Ruby Bee's mind, none of them kindly. She held them back, though, and it was just as well when Estelle finally produced a chunk of brick, dropped it back in the hole, stood up, and pointed her finger like she thought she was the high and mighty leader of an expedition.

"Start digging over there, Ruby Bee," she said, "and don't worry about them seeing us from inside the house. I told you time and again, they're both blind."